THE TOMB OF PTAHMES

C.W. JAMES

For information contact:

Insundry Productions Books, Gardnerville NV 89460

insundryproductions.com

Cover Design by Miblart.com

ISBN (ebook): 978-1-962056-04-5

ISBN (paperback): 978-1-962056-05-2

ISBN (hardback): 978-1-962056-06-9

Library of Congress Control Number: 2024909179

Also by C.W. James

The Treasure of Peril Island

Brothers Three

Mindfield

Special Thanks to
Ambrose Pratt

CHAPTER ONE

The scorpion walked across Carter Pinsent's foot. The seventeen-year-old put aside his pen and stretched, observing the arachnid's slow movements along the tent floor. He grabbed a nearby box, dumped out the pencils and quickly trapped the scorpion underneath it, as it angrily struck its cardboard prison. On his hands and knees, Carter maneuvered the box towards the opening of the tent flap. Once outside, he flipped the box and watched the scorpion scurry off into the sand.

The day's heat met him like a wall. Carter stood, gazing around the vast Libyan Desert, an infinite expanse of sandy nothingness, a captivating combination of beauty, isolated loneliness—and death. The sand was warm and gritty, with the smallest grains abrasive and coarse. The rolling dunes—big, endless, blown into swirling drifts and carved into patterns by the wind—reached up to scrape against a deep-blue sky, punctuated here and there by rocky outcroppings.

Carter inhaled, taking in the hot smell of the land. The eternal desert. It wasn't the same as being home in England, but the eternal sands hadn't changed since the last time he was here, a year ago... or, for that matter, eons. The breeze shifted and carried to him the camp aromas of donkey, sweat and faint hints of today's dinner.

He stepped back into the tent, his six-foot height barely brushing the canvas roof. The inside was not only hot, but stifling as well. There was no need to read the thermometer hanging on the nearby pole; he was positive the mercury registered over the 100-degree mark, as usual.

Carter had completely unbuttoned and untucked his shirt to give himself some relief from the high temperature. It was a chance he took. He hoped that his father, occupied with his own work, wouldn't pop in unexpectedly, take a glance at his half-nakedness and launch into his "we must maintain proper decorum even if we are not at home in London" speeches.

Good Lord! Carter thought, *this is 1910, after all! We're a decade into the twentieth century!*

Returning to the table, he continued his task of translating the inscription of a small stele, a stone slab, dating from the reign of Amenhotep III, around 1382 BC. His translation was almost complete, so it didn't take much time for him to finish. Now to present his effort to his father for approval.

He got up, buttoned his white shirt, all except the top three, and left the long sleeves rolled up above his elbows. Thankful that he absolutely refused to wear a tie, at least, he tucked in his shirt. He put on his solar topee, tilting it at a rakish angle. Picking up his translation, he stepped through the tent flaps.

The usually bustling and dusty archaeological dig site, located just outside the small town of Méydûm, was quiet this late in the day. Wooden stakes and string marked off the boundaries of the excavation area. Some open pits revealed the foundations of ancient stone walls, phantoms of the magnificent buildings which stood on this spot thousands of years ago. Tents and makeshift shelters dotted the area, where Carter, his archaeologist father and their Arab workers could rest, eat and store their equipment.

Carter rounded the corner of the tent and walked toward the one where his father worked, almost colliding with Migdal Abu, the Arab in charge of the workmen. "As-salamu alaykum."

"Wa alaykum as-salam," Migdal replied.

The two chatted about the day's activities, switching between English and Arabic, before they parted. Carter continued to another shelter, a tent with its sides rolled up and open to the air, crates full of objects from the excavation piled under the roof. In the center, his father bent over the table, whisking sand and dirt off a small statue with a brush.

"I completed the translation of the stele." Carter stepped up to his father and held out his work, almost like turning in homework to one of his school masters. He gave a slight shrug. "It's only about boundary marking."

Malcolm Pinsent took the offered page and adjusted his gold wire-rimmed glasses as he read the document. "That was quick."

"I always say hieroglyphs are my second language, if you don't count Arabic." Carter grinned.

There was once a time when Carter's father would have returned the grin or chuckled, but no longer. The reason sat on the table in a small frame. It held a photo of a beautiful woman, her vitality bursting from the two-dimensional image. Her red hair and blue eyes, traits Carter inherited, blazed out of the black-and-white picture. After her death, his father retreated into a permanent state of glumness, so much so that Carter now preferred staying at school, including most holidays.

"Well done, as usual." Mr. Pinsent removed his glasses and placed them and the paper on the table. "That will at least... yes?" Migdal Abu appeared in the shelter, quite excited. "What do you want, Migdal?"

Migdal bent almost double. "A thousand pardons—a white sheik has come riding on an ass, and with him a shameless female, also white."

"The dickens!" Carter said. Aside from his father, he had not seen another European for six weeks.

Migdal Abu advanced with hand outstretched. "He would have me give you this."

Mr. Pinsent took "this"... it was a calling card.

"How pompous! A carte-de-visite! And here we are—in the heart of the Libyan desert!" Carter laughed as he took the card his father held out after he glanced at it. The laughter stopped when Carter read what was printed on the pasteboard. "Sir Robert Ottley!"

He recognized the name: Ottley the great Egyptologist. Ottley the famous explorer. Ottley the eminent decipherer of cuneiform inscriptions.

Mr. Pinsent stood. He was half a head shorter than his son, but they both shared the same sharp features. "Sir Robert has in a few short years more than doubled the common stock of knowledge on the history of the Shepherd kings of the Nile. One must give him credit for that. His immense wealth grants him access to a wide array of artifacts, mostly without dealing with the trifling concerns of ethics, morals, or reportedly in a few cases, the law." He put on his solar topee. "Let us go and greet our guest. He arrives in the most appropriate mode of transportation possible. An ass riding on an ass."

Carter arched his eyebrows at his father's uncharacteristic snide remark and followed him. With Migdal leading the way, the trio went to the far side of the cluster of tents.

A little bronze-faced, grizzled old man attired from head to foot in glistening white duck and wearing on his head an enormous pith helmet. He possessed a large hawk-like nose, a small thin-lipped mouth and little eyes twinkling under beetled brows. He sat on a donkey that was already sound asleep, despite a plague of flies that buzzed about its eyes.

"Sir Robert Ottley," Father said with professional courtesy. "A thousand welcomes."

"You are very good," Sir Robert drawled. "I presume you are Mr. Malcolm Pinsent." He stooped a little forward and offered his hand.

"At your service." Mr. Pinsent shook his hand, then indicated Carter. "This is my son, Carter."

Carter bobbed his head.

"My daughter," Sir Robert said in slow, passionless tones. "Miss May Ottley."

Miss Ottley lifted her veil. Carter took a quick intake of breath. She was about his age, and, not only that, she was lovely. She smiled and showed a set of dazzling teeth. Carter was a shy idiot around pretty girls. A fact he confirmed when he swung off his hat and stammered some tardy words of welcome in a not quite coherent sentence.

"Will you not dismount and take some refreshment?" Mr. Pinsent asked in the same controlled voice Carter had heard him use while endeavoring to be polite with people he disliked.

"Thank you, no. I have come to ask a favor." Sir Robert glanced round him, the lord of the manor looking over his serf's land. "Where are your Arabs?"

Carter surveyed him in blank astonishment. *The arrogance! Our Arabs? Like we owned them?*

"They went to town for a well-deserved rest," Mr. Pinsent answered. "Why do ask?"

"I am camped on the southern slope of the Hill of Rakh," Sir Robert replied. "It is twelve miles distant. I have found the tomb for which I have been searching for years. I thought I had enough Arabs to finish the job. I was mistaken. I wish to borrow yours."

"The Arabs are not cattle to be driven from one pasture to another!" Carter blurted out. He was starting to join in his father's dislike of Sir Robert.

"My father was not implying—" Miss Ottley returned with the ferocity of a tiger.

"Now, now, dear." Sir Robert stopped her with a raised hand and turned to Carter with a smile. "You will forgive me? There was no personal reflection."

"You may have the use of my workers and welcome," Mr. Pinsent said.

"Suitably paid, of course," Carter lobbed in.

Miss Ottley sat erect in her saddle. "How dare you—"

Sir Robert calmed his daughter with another wave of his hand and chuckled as if Carter had made a joke. "By all means, your Arabs will be paid." He smiled again. For some reason, that smile pushed Carter backwards a step.

"We will send them to your encampment tomorrow morning," Carter's father said.

"I am immensely obliged to you, Mr. Pinsent." Sir Robert gave an odd little bow. "He gives twice who gives quickly. But I need their services immediately. The sarcophagus is in a rock hole forty feet beneath the level of the desert. I simply must have it up tonight."

"It's kind of you to allow us to help you at your triumph, but why does the work have to be done tonight? Is it the sarcophagus of a king?" Mr. Pinsent asked.

"No," said Miss Ottley, "a priest of Amen of the eighteenth dynasty."

"Oh, a priest." Carter's father was not impressed.

"No king was ever half as interesting as our priest." Miss Ottley gathered all her dignity, at least as much which can be had while seated on a donkey. She almost matched her father's haughtiness. "He was a wonderful man in every way, a prophet, a magician and enormously powerful. Besides, he is believed to have committed suicide for the sake of principle, and he predicted his own resurrection."

"Like Jesus of Nazareth?" Carter asked incredulously.

"Our priest did not claim divinity," Miss Ottley shot back.

"That's a relief." Carter grinned.

Miss Ottley bridled at Carter's tone. "He said he would return after a sleep of two thousand years."

"He's a trifle behind schedule, isn't he?" Carter remarked dryly.

"Is that his fault?" cried the girl.

"It falsifies his prophecy," Carter argued.

Both Mr. Pinsent and Sir Robert raised their hands, speaking simultaneously. "Children!"

Carter unnecessarily adjusted his hat and cleared his throat. He put his fists on his hips.

"His name was Ptahmes," Sir Robert turned his attention to Mr. Pinsent. "He was the right-hand man of Amenhotep IV. That king created a new monotheistic religion devoted to a single god named Aten, the sun god. Then he embarked on a widespread attempt to remove any signs of the traditional Egyptian deities.

Ptahmes apparently killed himself as a protest for the deposition of his particular divinity, Amen, the focus of the king's disapproval."

"Read that." Miss Ottley extracted a piece of paper from a saddlebag and thrust it out like a weapon.

Mr. Pinsent took it, glanced at it, then handed it to his son. "Read it out loud, please, Carter. I left my glasses in the tent."

Carter looked at the page of type-written manuscript. "'Hearken to the orders which are put upon you by Ptahmes, named Tahutimes, son of Mery, son of Hap. All my ways were regulated even as the pace of an ibis. The Hawk-headed Horus was my protector like amulets upon my body. I trained the troops of my lord. I made his pylon sixty cubits long in the noble rock of quartzite, most great in height and firm as heaven. I did not imitate what had been done before.

"I was the royal scribe of the recruits. Mustering was done under me. I was appointed Judge of the Palace, overseer of all the prophets of the south and of the north. I was appointed High Priest of Amen in the Capital—King of all the Gods. I was made the eyes and ears of the king: keeper of my lord's heart and fan-bearer at the King's right hand. Great men have come from afar to bow themselves before me, bringing presents of ivory and gold, copper, silver and emery, lazuli, malachite, green feldspar and vases of mern wood inlaid with white precious stones sometimes bearing gold at one time 1000 deben.'" He cast a questioning glance toward his father.

"About 200 pounds in weight," Mr. Pinsent said.

"Quite a sizable amount." Carter went on, "'For my fame was carried abroad even as the fame of the king, 'lord of the sweet wind.' And there was spoken of me by the son of Paapis that my wisdom was of a divine nature, because of my knowledge of futurities. Yet on the sixth day of the month of Pakhons in the 18th year I desire to rest.

"My lord, at the solicitation of the great royal wife and mother Nefertiti, has put off the worship of his predecessors. The name of Amen is proscribed from the country. Ra is proscribed from the country. Horus is proscribed from the country. Aten is set up in their place and worshiped in the land. My lord has even changed his name. Apiy is the high priest of the new God that is from the Mesopotamian wilderness. Amen, king of the Gods, dandled my lord and is forsaken and proscribed."

"I am an old man and would rest: although my lord has not forsaken me. He has appointed me overseer of all his works. Therefore, shall you carry me to the temple of Kak, and give my body to the hands of the priests of Amen who will wrap me in the linen sheets of Horus without removing my heart, my entrails or my lungs.'" Carter looked up. "That's odd for ancient Egyptian burial practice. The internal organs were usually removed, embalmed separately and placed in canopic jars."

"You are correct, my lad, the request was indeed out of the norm," Sir Robert said. "Pray continue."

Carter nodded. "'Then you shall carry me to Khizebh and enclose me in the place prepared for me; and cover my tomb to a depth of five fathoms with the sand of the desert at that hour when no man looks or listens. Do this even as I command, and as royal scribe I trace the order with my pen. But you shall place my papyri and the sign by which I shall be known, and the stele of ivory engraved with the directions to the priests of Amen who are to wake me from my sleep at the distant hour, in the tomb that is prepared for my body in the temple of Merenptah and in such manner that I shall there appear to sleep.

"And all these things you shall do, or my curse shall pursue you and your children and their children for the space of four hundred lives. Nor shall you remove the endowment of my gifts nor touch them where they lie under a penalty of great wrath.'"

Carter strained his eyes to read the last words, tilting the paper to catch the remaining light as the darkness was already setting down upon the desert. "That is most interesting," Carter said, tendering the document to Miss Ottley with the care of feeding a crocodile. "Isn't it, Father?"

"Very," Mr. Pinsent nodded. "From a papyrus, of course?"

"Yes," Sir Robert's daughter replied, "as well as an ivory stele. Father came into possession of them a few years ago."

"Oh, I had not heard." Suspicion tinged Mr. Pinsent's voice. It seemed to Carter he was about to witness a fencing match without the use of foils.

Sir Robert coughed. "No, nor anyone else. I have never published it. It did not come to me in the usual way. I bought it from an Arab who had rifled the tomb in which it was discovered."

"And the other papyri and the ivory stele," Carter's father said, "they enabled you to locate the real location that holds the body?"

"They assisted." Then silence supervened. At length Sir Robert cleared his throat and spoke. "There were reasons why I should not broadcast the find abroad."

"No doubt," Mr. Pinsent said, with intentioned dryness.

"One papyrus speaks of a golden treasure," Sir Robert went on quietly. "If published, it would have set thousands looking for the tomb. Archaeologists frequently are viewed as 'grave robbers.' No need to provide directions for the real ones. The body of Ptahmes could be destroyed by some vandal intent solely on pillage."

"You assumed a large responsibility," Mr. Pinsent said.

"Do you dispute my right?" he said coldly.

Mr. Pinsent shrugged his shoulders. "It is not for me to say, Sir Robert. I am sure you will be able to satisfy the Royal Society and other authorities that you have acted rightly. When the time comes."

"I admit no responsibility," Sir Robert answered, "and permit me to observe that you are talking nonsense. I owe no duty to communicate the results of my purchases or discoveries to any group or to the world."

Mr. Pinsent nodded. "True, Sir Robert. An action for damages could not lie against you."

"Sir!" The Egyptologist cried in anger.

"Father," said Miss Ottley, "how can Mr. Pinsent's foolish sarcasm affect you? Besides, we need his Arabs."

"Quite so. We need his Arabs." Sir Robert flashed one of his smiles. "And if you require a reward for the courtesy we asked and you promised of your own accord, you have but to name a sum in cash to have it paid."

The cool impudence of the pair struck Carter dumb. He sputtered, working hard to suppress the urge to drag the great Sir Robert Ottley off his donkey and shove that sanctimonious face of his into the sand. "There is no need. My father is a man of honor and his word."

Mr. Pinsent gave Carter an appreciative nod, and continued, his voice controlled and even. "You may use my workers, with pay, as I have previously offered. Carter, please give Migdal the necessary instructions."

"Yes, sir," Carter grumbled. Switching into Arabic, he directed Migdal to gather their workers from town and take them to Sir Robert's camp. He added to make sure they see the money before allowing the work to begin.

Carter and Migdal exchanged glances. It was clear the two shared the same opinion of Ottley. Migdal bowed. "Ana afham." He left.

"I am obliged to you, Mr. Pinsent," said Sir Robert. He looked at the sky. "How brightly the stars will shine tonight."

Without another word, Sir Robert dragged the head of his donkey round and set out for his camp. His daughter followed. Carter and his father watched in silence as they rode away. Finally, Carter spoke.

"Why would he withhold so valuable a historic discovery for so many years from the world?" he asked. "Isn't such a course of action opposed to all practice of scientific research? Do you believe his story about the treasure to be the reason?"

"A great number of the ancient tombs have been plundered down the ages, so I suppose it is plausible." Carter's father shrugged again. "But it is at odds, too, with the man's reputed character. It would have covered him with glory if he placed his discovery before the Society we both belong to. There are a dozen incidents related to him proving that he is not, shall we say, indifferent to praise and fame. I just don't know."

Father turned and walked back toward the work tent. Carter stared after the receding figures of Sir Robert and Miss Ottley. The setting sun transformed the sand into a sea of blood.

CHAPTER TWO

Carter slowly stepped closer to the sarcophagus, squinting his eyes in the dim light. He could make out the mummy's leathery skin crinkling at its joints and shriveled eyeballs set deep into its skull. A smell like ancient books filled the room as he studied the body—one that had been shrouded in death for centuries.

A searing blast of red light emanated from within the sarcophagus, momentarily blinding Carter. When his vision cleared, he could make out the form of the mummy again, but its eyes were open, two obsidian pools staring back at him with a frightening intensity. And then the wrapped figure spoke—or rather, croaked—in a dry and rasping voice, forming one sole word: "Pinsent."

Carter jolted awake, feeling a sense of dread that seemed to encompass the entirety of his tent. He held his breath and listened intently, worrying something was lurking in the darkness, and expected to hear his name called by that unearthly voice once more. After several moments he let out a shaky sigh of relief, embarrassed at himself for overreacting to a dream.

A voice whispered his name urgently. "Mr. Pinsent! Mr. Pinsent!"

Carter gasped, then grinned. That was real, not from a nightmare. He blinked and rubbed his eyes, fumbling for the matchbox on the table next to his cot. He struck a light, the flame providing a small circle of brightness in the darkness of the tent. His bare feet touched the cold sand as he pulled on his trousers then opened the tent flap. An Arab scurried past in the half-light, a tangle of robes billowing behind him.

"Hello!" Carter made a grab at the passing figure. "Not so fast, my man."

"It is I—May Ottley," Carter's visitor replied.

"Miss Ottley!" Carter stepped back, bewildered.

Her black hair was tucked away under a long, tan-colored turban. She wore a weatherworn burnous, its once pristine white hue now dulled from the sun and sand, and she tightly clutched it around her body to ward off the chill of evening. Her eyes drooped with exhaustion as she lowered herself onto a campstool. "May I have a drink of water?"

"Yes, of course." Carter poured some from the small bottle by his cot into a tin cup and handed it to her. "Is anything wrong?"

She drained the cup before answering. Despite her evident fatigue and upset, her response was terse and business-like. "Yes."

It was apparent she wasn't going to elaborate. "I'll get my father." He jogged to the next tent and went inside. "Father! Father!"

Mr. Pinsent groaned, stirred and opened his eyes.

"Miss Ottley's in my tent." Carter gestured toward it.

"What?" Mr. Pinsent struggled with the cover to sit up in the cot.

"She seems to be in some distress. Something must have happened at Sir Robert's camp," Carter explained. "I think she was looking for you and came into my tent by mistake."

"Give me a minute." Mr. Pinsent gave a begrudging nod, and Carter stepped outside to wait. His father emerged a few moments later, buttoning his coat while throwing an irritated glance at Carter. With an uncomfortable flicker of embarrassment, Carter realized he had neglected to finish dressing.

Carter and his father hurried back to his tent. As they arrived, he held the flap open for his father to enter first. Miss Ottley was dozing in the camp chair. Carter touched her shoulder, and she jolted awake, eyes wide with shock. Carter caught the cup she flung in mid-air as it went flying across the tent.

"Now,"—Carter put down the cup—"my father is here. Tell us what happened."

"It was a bad thing," she began. "The sarcophagus was filled with treasure, gold and silver in bars, and other things. The Arabs went mad. My father fought like a paladin and held them off for a day and a half. But soon after dark, this evening a caravan arrived. The fight was renewed, and my father was wounded. The Arabs secured the treasure and fled into the desert. Our dragoman was the only one who kept faith in us. He has gone by the river to Khonsu for troops. I hurried here for you. I ran almost all the way. Will you come? My father is very ill… injured. He has lost a lot of blood. He was shot in the shoulder."

Mr. Pinsent was quiet for a moment. "I am not a medical man, Miss Ottley, but I have had some experience with first aid. Let me gather my supplies, then we will accompany you back to your camp and I'll see what I can do. Carter, ready the donkeys."

Carter sprinted out of the tent. He flew to the makeshift corral and quickly saddled the donkeys. Within ten minutes, he had them hitched up and ready to go. Miss Ottley waited by the entrance of the tent, her jaw set with determination. Carter noticed that his father now wore a holster snugly attached to his hip.

Mr. Pinsent helped Miss Ottley onto a donkey and turned to Carter. "Finish getting ready and follow us." As Carter turned to leave, his father grabbed his shoulder. "Armed," he added in a quiet command.

Carter nodded, then returned to his tent and finished dressing. He reached into his trunk, his fingers curling around the cold metal of his gun. A strange mix of dread and anticipation filled him as he loaded the revolver—the thrill of an unknown adventure combined with a fearful anxiety—a soldier marching towards his ultimate fate on a battlefield. He strapped on his holster and went outside.

He grabbed a handful of mane as he yanked himself atop the donkey, which gave a low grumble of protest. Kicking the animal into a faster trot, he trailed after the others. He eventually caught up to Miss Ottley, only to find her focused on the horizon ahead, completely ignoring his presence. The wooden saddle creaked in time with the animal's plodding steps as they rode side by side in silence, Carter unable to decide if it would be appropriate to talk with her or not. He finally mustered the courage to at least try.

"You must have done that twelve miles in record time. It is not yet one o'clock," he said.

"I made it in six hours, I think," she replied.

"You are an athlete, by Jove!"

"I am no bread-and-butter miss, at any rate."

Carter wanted to keep the conversation going, but it appeared it was over. With a combination of embarrassment and annoyance, he let his donkey lag behind, becoming the last in a single file.

All around the three riders the desert stretched out in its infinite expanse, vast and empty. The stars dotted the night sky, searing pinpricks of light, and a cool breeze blew up from the nearby Nile. The distant whoop of a hyena echoed through the stillness of the early morning air, and everything seemed to be shrouded in an ethereal veil of silence and mystery. Carter knew he was falling deeper and deeper under Egypt's spell, captivated by her beauty and grandeur, her sorrowful secrets and ancient riddles. He understood how no other place had ever called to his parents, and him, in such a way.

The trio arrived an hour later at the mountain. Miss Ottley slipped off her donkey. "This way, Mr. Pinsent."

Carter slid off his donkey and gathered the reins of all three. "I'll take care of them."

"Excellent. Join us when you've finished." Mr. Pinsent leaned in slightly and spoke in a low tone. "And keep your eyes open."

Carter nodded. Miss Ottley and his father hurried away through the smaller of the three pylons that fronted a small temple hollowed out of the rock face of the hill.

The Ottley camp was small, with only three or four tents in varying shades of brown and green along the western edge. Sir Robert's supplies were nowhere to be seen, likely kept safe inside the temple. Carter secured the donkeys to a line of stakes driven into the ground, his gaze roving the area for any signs of movement or danger. He trailed behind the others as they entered the temple, one hand on his gun just in case.

He had to crouch down and squeeze himself through the small, low stone doorway. The corridor was narrow, the walls made of cold, hard rock, cracked in several places. He followed a light at the end of the tunnel until he reached another doorway. He entered the chamber and it seemed as if it had been struck by a vicious earthquake: tools lay scattered all over the floor, two tables stood lopsided against one wall, maps, journals and other exploration materials strewn across the ground. In the dim light, another opening loomed in the back wall, its darkness a portal into the unknown.

Sir Robert Ottley lay among the chaos on the floor. He was evidently unconscious, and with a high fever. Carter's father knelt next to him, a lamp held in one hand.

"There is an oil stove in the corner, Carter. Please light it and boil some water," Mr. Pinsent crisply directed.

Carter lit the stove, then dashed out of the temple, frantically searching for some kind of vessel, eventually finding an old pot. He returned to the temple, filled the pot with water from a wooden bucket in the corner, and placed it on top of the stove. His father had already set up a workstation on a threadbare towel spread across the floor, pulling out metal tools, tweezers and bottles of dark liquids from a worn, brown Gladstone bag.

Miss Ottley watched with an expression Carter would never forget. Her face was as pale as a ghost. Her big red-brown eyes glowed like coals and were ringed with purple hollows. She was manifestly worn out and on the verge of a breakdown.

"I understand your concern over Sir Robert's condition, but I think it would be best if you retired, Miss Ottley," Mr. Pinsent said.

"No. I shall remain." Her response was curt and clipped.

"Miss Ottley," Carter's father firmly repeated, "I am not a doctor, and although I am prepared to do the best I can, I don't pretend to be able to do the impossible. You are strung up to more than concert pitch. Without rest, you'll break down altogether. Your hovering over me is distracting. I shall not answer for your father's life if you force me to nurse two patients at once."

Miss Ottley shook her head.

Mr. Pinsent began examining Sir Robert's wound. "Carter, please assist Miss Ottley to her tent."

"Miss Ottley." Carter held out one hand.

She took a step back. "No. I shall remain."

Carter judged by her eyes that she had become his enemy, and a critical enemy at that. "Miss Ottley—"

She shook her head again.

"Carter!" Mr. Pinsent barked. "Kindly remove her!"

"I'm trying!"

"Well, try harder," his father ordered.

"Try harder. Right," Carter muttered under his breath. He walked over to Miss Ottley. He took her by one arm and attempted to turn her toward the exit. She yanked her arm out of his grip, glaring at him. With a determined sigh, he picked her up in his arms and carried her struggling like a wildcat to the door. When they reached outside the temple, he put her down and blocked the entrance.

She charged forward, desperate to get past Carter and back inside. But he stood firm, blocking her path with a menacing arm as she pushed against him in vain. His eyes glowed with intense determination, daring her to continue.

"You heard my father." Carter failed to keep the irritation out of his voice. "You must have some rest. You cannot do anything more for Sir Robert at present. Please go to your tent."

Her eyes flashed and her jaw clenched as she hissed at Carter, "I am not your servant to obey your orders!"

"At present, you are."

"My place is by my father!" She tried to duck under his arm and dart past him, but he blocked her every move with an outstretched arm and the solid wall of his hips. She let out a low growl of frustration before finally giving up. They stood toe-to-toe.

"Please go to your tent," Carter said.

"I hate you!" she spat out, then slapped him.

Carter's mind raced with a flurry of responses, but it seemed to him this was one of those occasions where silence was golden. He kept his mouth firmly shut.

When she started to cry, Carter was at a loss. He didn't know what to do so he stood still and watched her. As the tears eventually stopped, he couldn't help but notice how beautiful she was; from the little Grecian nose to the round chin, every feature was exquisite. Yet at the same time, he could sense her immense pride at being Sir Robert Ottley's daughter.

Carter spoke in a calm, soothing voice, but underlined each word. "Miss Ottley, my father will do all that is within his power to help Sir Robert. At least he will try to get him stabilized until your dragoman returns and your father is taken for proper medical assistance. You may count on that. He is also correct in that you must rest. We will let you know of any changes in his condition."

She nodded and went off as meek as any lamb toward one of the tents. Carter stayed on watch for a few minutes until he was convinced Miss Ottley wouldn't reappear. He went back into the temple. His father was on his feet by Sir Robert, wiping his hands on a bloody towel.

"How is he?" Carter asked.

Mr. Pinsent shrugged. "I managed to remove the bullet from under his clavicle, and then dressed the wound and bound him up. I gave him a hypodermic dose of morphia, and he dropped asleep. My big worry is infection." He gestured around the rocky chamber. "This isn't the most sterile of locations. What about his daughter?"

"She finally retired to her tent." Carter went on with a grin. "I must admit, for a while I felt I was back at school in a rugger match."

His father's expression did not change. "Let's carry him into his tent. I'd rather he rest in his cot than on a cold stone floor. Take his feet."

Carter picked up Sir Robert's feet while his father gingerly lifted him by his shoulders. The two carried the prostrate form to the tent Carter indicated with a nod. They lay their patient on his cot.

"I will take the first watch." Mr. Pinsent wearily sat on a camp-stool. "Please return in four hours."

"Yes, sir," Carter replied. "I think I'll go look at the sarcophagus, since it's been the cause of this little incident."

Mr. Pinsent returned a gruff nod, and Carter headed out of the tent. In the east, a deep scarlet hue crept across the horizon as dawn neared. He stole a glance at Miss Ottley's tent. It was silent, so he returned to the temple. Once inside the first chamber, he lifted the lantern and scanned the room.

The walls were plain and sterile, not even a trace of hiero-glyphics or murals. The only items present were Sir Robert's tools and notes. No wonder they hadn't discovered anything remark-able—there was nothing to find.

Carter automatically straightened the place up a little. He right-ed one table, collected a few of the journals and notes, placing them on top. He glanced at the dark doorway leading to the rest of the tomb and lit a lantern. Taking swift strides, he entered the second chamber, about the same size as the first. His gaze swept over walls that were also strangely empty of any artwork before he let out a soft gasp of surprise.

His eyes were drawn to the wooden scaffolding dominating the middle of the space. It was fixed with hooks, cables and ropes, supporting it over a deep cavity in the floor. Next to the pit, he saw a gargantuan sarcophagus that instantly piqued his interest. He walked up to it, fascinated. It was completely made of lead, an element that was uncommon for tombs such as this one. The box was totally bare, not decorated in any way, unlike many other sarcophagi he'd seen.

Carter began to check inside but stopped as the memory of the dream he had returned. "Stop being silly," he said under his breath. He looked in. It was empty.

He surveyed his surroundings. The lid of the sarcophagus lay propped against a pillar. Carved in perfect detail was the figure and face of a tall, austere man. Carter brought the lantern closer, causing erratic shadows to dance across the sculpture's features. The soft flicker of light and shifting shadows gave the impression that the engraved image was almost alive.

"So you're old Ptahmes." Carter gave a salute. "How do you do? Now where is your mummy, old chap?"

Carter turned a full circle, scanning the room. Aside from the wooden scaffolding and the large sarcophagus, there was nothing else in sight. He made his way toward the deep pit in the middle of the chamber and tested one of the legs of the scaffolding for stability. After finding it solid enough he grasped one leg and slowly leaned over the edge, holding out his lantern in front of him.

The pit was as empty as the sarcophagus.

With a sigh, he pulled himself back from the edge. The workers could have taken the mummy when they stole the gold, he thought. After all, there is a black market for Egyptian artifacts. He shook his head. Why bother with a mummy that was worth a fraction of all the treasure they plundered?

His thoughts drifted to Sir Robert and Miss Ottley. How devastating it must have been for them to find the tomb they had been searching for for years, only to have the treasure stolen, and find the burial chamber empty. Not even Ptahmes' mummy present... their quest only yielded an empty lead box.

Carter returned to the first chamber. He stopped at a slight noise coming from behind him—like someone or something was scratching in the darkened room he just left.

"Must be an animal," he mumbled to himself, but decided to check just the same.

He strode back into the second chamber, his booted feet echoing on the hard stone floor. The area was as lifeless as it was before. He inspected every inch of the walls, even crouching down to check for any chinks or cracks that could give a creature passage into the room. Cautiously, he moved closer to the pit and squinted at its black depths; it was still empty save for some forgotten debris strewn across the bottom.

Carter shrugged, then a chill ran up his spine. "Somebody walking over my grave," he muttered. He was sure he saw movement out of the corner of his eye, and he spun toward it. A dark shape stood by the sarcophagus. It seemed to be shaped like a man, but its back was presented to Carter.

"What the deuce are you doing here, whoever you are?" Carter cried out and started forward. He pulled out his revolver with his free hand. "Answer me!"

The shape melted in an instant into thinnest air.

CHAPTER THREE

C arter stared at the empty space for almost a minute in confusion.

"It must have been a shadow." He stumbled over his words, trying to make sense of what he had seen.

The figure he saw had appeared so solid and real but had dissolved into nothingness. His mind raced through all the possibilities of what it could have been. A shadow? It couldn't be anything else, since that was the only rational and scientific explanation available. But how could that explain the tangible presence he believed—no, he saw—only moments ago? He stood for a long while in confusion and disbelief. And if it had been a shadow, what threw it?

The lantern in Carter's hand lit up the room, but still the walls remained dull and brown. It couldn't have been his own shadow, thrown by reflection. No other light source illuminated this space or the room behind him.

Perhaps there might be a secret entrance to the chamber, and some robber acquainted with it might be employing it, Carter reasoned. He embarked on a second tour of the walls and examined them intently, but was forced to abandon that idea like the other one. As he stood in the center of the tomb, trying to come up with yet another possible explanation, he sensed another presence—there was someone, or something, in here with him.

Carter pulled out his gun. His finger twitched and he cocked the gun without any conscious thought. He knew that shooting inside could result in being hit by a ricochet, but the cold, deadly weight of the weapon gave him a feeling of security.

He backed out of the chamber as though retreating from a gang of thieves wielding drawn scimitars. He extinguished his lantern and fled down the entry hall as he glanced over his shoulder to make sure there were no pursuers. Once outside in the blazing desert sun, he released a deep sigh of relief and chuckled as he placed his gun back into its holster. He turned down the lantern and set it on the ground.

Just a shadow...

Carter glanced around the camp and found the storehouse and kitchen in the third tent—a blessing that the robbers were only after gold and left the stores. He built a fire and prepared a simple meal of coffee and curry for himself, his father and Miss Ottley. He boiled some beef broth for the invalid, poured it into a bowl and set it on a tray. Then he carried it with the tea back to Sir Robert's tent.

"Father?" Carter slipped through the tent flaps.

His father gazed into the distance, lost in thought. Carter's guilt at not being at his mother's side during her final moments resurfaced, fueled by the hospital nurses' words about how his father refused to leave her, even to eat. But a voice inside reminded Carter that he couldn't have been there, no matter what. It was the fault of the railway company and delayed trains for keeping him away. He knew that was the rational excuse, the obvious truth. But it didn't help much.

Carter cleared his throat. "Father?" Mr. Pinsent started a little, then gazed at his son. Carter offered the tray. "I made something to eat, and some beef tea for Sir Robert, if he can take anything."

"Thank you." Mr. Pinsent took the tray and set it on a small nightstand. He picked up the cup.

"How's Sir Robert doing?" Carter looked down at the figure on the cot.

"He woke briefly about an hour ago." Mr. Pinsent took a sip of coffee. "Although a little feverish, I am quite satisfied with his progress."

"That's good to hear. I'll take Miss Ottley her meal, then I'll return and give you a break." His father nodded. Carter returned to the cook tent to dish up another bowl of curry and pour another cup of coffee. He took them to Miss Ottley's tent. "Miss Ottley?" he called in as he stood outside. "Are you awake?"

"Yes." A tired voice came from inside.

"I brought you something to eat and a cup of coffee. I thought you might be hungry."

"Come in."

Carter backed his way through the flaps. Miss Ottley sat on the edge of her cot, staring blankly in front of her. He set the bowl and cup on a trunk next to the cot, then gestured toward the food and flashed an awkward smile. "Curry and coffee. My specialty." He tried again, adding what he hoped was some levity. "Fall to and repair your waste tissues. That's an order. In plain English—eat."

"Thank you." Her voice was weary and flat.

After a pause, Carter spoke again. "I'm sorry about that business at the temple. I mean, carrying you out and blocking your return. But—"

"You were merely doing what you were told," she replied. She didn't need to add the rest of the unspoken sentence: like a good little soldier.

Carter felt his temper rising at her implication. "My father did what he believed was best for Sir Robert at the time," he said with some irritation, "and I agreed with him." He didn't know what to say beyond that, so turned to leave.

"He's dead, I think," Miss Ottley whispered.

Carter took a hesitant step towards her, feeling guilty for having raised his voice before. "No, no. My father believes Sir Robert has been through the worst and will remain stable until your drago-man arrives to get him to proper medical assistance."

She shook her head, still not looking at him. "No—he died, for all intents and purposes, the hour he was shot. His heart and soul are wrapped up in his work. His terrible disappointment has deprived him of his best support."

"The robbery, you mean?"

"No, not that—the knowledge of his failure. Our failure." Miss Ottley was gazing at the ground with a face of marble, but tears trickled from her eyes. "He was certain of finding the mummy of Ptahmes."

"Ah!" Carter replied, and promptly ran out of words. He decided he should change the subject, try to steer her mind away from her father's health and towards something else. His eyes flitted towards the small table in the corner of the tent, covered with stacks of papers of hieroglyphs.

"I see you must do translations. So do I. My second language is hieroglyphs if you don't count Arabic! I always say that!" He grinned. Despite sensing her lack of enthusiasm for the conversation, he plowed on. "I find Hieratic can be quite a challenge, though. The individual symbols are often connected and flow together like handwriting. I mean, it is handwriting... ancient Egyptian script. Not to mention all the possible individual variations and abbreviations, which differ from standard hieroglyphic forms. It makes translation much harder, don't you think?"

He might as well have been trying to converse with the sphinx. He gave up. "Try to eat something. It will make you feel better."

Stepping out of her tent, he returned to Sir Robert's. He was glad to see that his father had eaten the curry.

"I appreciated the food," Mr. Pinsent said. "Sir Robert awoke enough for me to give him some of your beef tea. He pronounced it 'muck'."

Carter chuckled. "He must be improving."

A faint smile tugged at the corners of his father's lips, the first one Carter had seen in a long time. Mr. Pinsent stood and stretched, and for a split second there was the hope of warmth in the air, but then his father's expression hardened, as though recalling a memory. "We may be past the crisis. Perhaps. But there's no way of telling. The doctors say a patient is improving, but then…" His voice grew thick with bitterness, leaving Carter feeling helpless and uneasy.

"Let's pray all will be well," Carter said quietly.

"Pray." Mr. Pinsent spat out the word with disgust. He sighed. "I need to return to our camp to replenish my medical supplies in case he takes a turn for the worse, or the dragoman takes longer to return than expected. Or perhaps he doesn't return at all, if he's in league with the robbers. I need you to sit with Sir Robert."

"Of course." Carter cast an anxious glance toward his patient. "What do I do if…"

"There is aspirin powder in that package on the table. If his fever gets higher, dissolve it in a glass of water and get it down him, no matter how he fights," Mr. Pinsent said. "If it is a very high temperature, soak some towels in water and lay them on him. I hope to be back in a few hours, if the donkey cooperates."

"I understand."

"Good. I know I can count on you." Mr. Pinsent clamped his hand on Carter's shoulder as he passed on his way out of the tent. "So like your mother."

Carter pushed down the lump in his throat, then paused for a brief moment before picking up a two-week old issue of a Cairo newspaper and seating himself on the campstool. He forced himself to read each article, even if it wasn't interesting to him. Ten minutes dragged by in agonizingly silent stillness, save for the crinkling noises from his turning the pages. Suddenly, without warning, Sir Robert's eyes snapped open and he uttered an incomprehensible sound.

Putting the newspaper aside, Carter bent over him. Their eyes met. There was the light of reason in them. Carter didn't know why, but he pressed Sir Robert's hand, then remembered the words Miss Ottley had said about the importance of her father's work.

"You must hurry up and get well, Sir Robert," Carter said in the brisk, cheerful tones of a visitor to the sickroom, "or I shall not be able to contain my curiosity. This Ptahmes of yours is the most extraordinary mummy I have ever heard of. I am excited to see him taken from his shroud."

The eyes of the wounded man actually glowed. His fingers clutched at Carter's wrist, and with a superhuman effort he gasped forth, "No—no."

"Rest easy," Carter returned, "Nobody will touch him until you are well. But you must hurry. Remember we are of a trade, all three of us. You, my father and I."

Sir Robert appeared relieved and very slowly his eyes closed. His breathing was imperceptible. For one horrible moment, Carter thought his patient had died. He felt for a pulse and found it. Although faint, it was regular. Carter returned to the paper. Out of sheer desperation, he began to read the section about shipping news.

"The cat!"

Carter gasped at the cry, the paper crumpling under his grip. Sir Robert lay in his cot, eyes wide open and blazing with fear. His trembling index finger pointed at something behind Carter, who slowly turned to find an empty corner of the tent.

"The cat!" Sir Robert repeated more urgently. "There! Over there! Black as Erebus with flaming yellow eyes!"

Carter looked again over his shoulder. As before, there was nothing there. He tried to make light of it. "Well, that's a good omen, isn't it? Cats were considered symbols of protection and deities in ancient—"

"The cat!" Sir Robert grew more agitated.

Carter stood and figured that the best course of action would be to play along. With exaggerated motions of his arms, he began to imitate herding a cat out of the tent. He stamped his feet on the ground and clapped his hands together. "Scat! Shoo! Go away! That's it, scat!" His voice grew louder as he shuffled towards the entrance, flapping the tent flap open with a final emphatic shout of "shoo!"

Miss Ottley stood on the other side.

Carter felt his cheeks flush. "Ah, Sir Robert thought he saw a cat and was getting worked up about it. So I tried to reassure him," he said as he turned to glance towards Miss Ottley's father who had drifted off to sleep again. He gave an embarrassed shrug. "Maybe it was all a dream..."

"I shall sit with my father." It was not a request. It was a dismissal.

Carter said nothing and stepped outside. After Miss Ottley went in, he swept off his solar topee and performed an exaggerated bow. "As you wish, your highness," he muttered.

He straightened up, placed his hat back atop his head and planted his fists on his hips. After a second's contemplation, he decided to get a cup of coffee. As he started for the cook tent, his gaze shifted to the opening of the temple. Curiosity about the peculiar coffin and tomb tugged at him again. Taking up the lamp once more, he ventured into the first room and stopped to survey it.

Carter had been in tombs before; he helped his parents excavate one along the Nile three years ago. But this one was different. Master builders and supervisors performed rituals during construction and guidelines were provided on where to build, how to design, even what materials to use. Ancient Egyptians thought of tombs as 'houses of eternity'. He sometimes felt as if he was an unwelcome trespasser in somebody's home when he entered other tombs. But how could the vast empty spaces of knowledge about the distant past be filled without doing so?

He should be standing in the mortuary chapel, a room accessible to visitors to perform rites and make offerings of food and drink for the deceased. Usually false doors were also placed in these chapels to connect the worlds of the living and the dead, permitting the spirit of the person to move freely between the chapel and the tomb to receive offerings. However, this room was devoid of any indication of being intended for use in that way.

Nothing was written on the walls. Given Ptahmes' status, there should've been at least one cartouche of his name carved in the rock. No thief, no matter how greedy, could steal that. But the place was bare.

He stepped through the portal into the second chamber and stopped, looking about his feet. No debris, so the Ottleys didn't need to break in. A close examination of the doorway confirmed it had not been sealed, also very unusual.

Carter again scanned the walls, incredulous at the barren and dull interior, despite Ptahmes' importance as a priest. Normally, this type of tomb would be covered in intricate hieroglyphs extolling his accomplishments, along with incantations from the Book of the Dead. The walls should have been adorned with Ptahmes' titles and honors. Not here.

Ancient Egyptians were buried with at least some goods thought to be necessary after death. At a minimum, these were everyday objects such as bowls, combs and other trinkets, along with food. But again, they were missing here. There were no shabti figures—small figurines which were believed to come to life and perform any labor required by the deceased—or offering vessels or food. Even more unusual, no jewelry, amulets or personal belongings, such as clothing and furniture, were present.

Were those items stolen as well? But then, why would the grave robbers take such objects after their massive haul of treasure? This tomb seemed as if it had been given a thorough cleaning by the most conscientious housekeeper ever. Carter leaned against a wall as he thought things through.

The notion of an afterlife was very important to the ancient Egyptians. To them, life continued after death, and they devoted their lives to making sure that they would go smoothly into the hereafter. That was the reason their tombs were designed to keep the body intact and provide a comfortable atmosphere in which to spend their eternity. Why, then, did this tomb seem so at odds with all those strong, ancient Egyptian beliefs?

He straightened up when he recalled Ptahmes' prophecy: he would wake up after two thousand years' sleep. That could explain why the typical Egyptian tomb items weren't present. They were put in the tombs of the deceased to help them in the afterlife, but Ptahmes believed he had no need of them. He didn't plan on crossing the Duat—the river between this life and the next world. The plan was to return to this one. The door to this chamber was left unsealed so he could use it to reemerge to the outside.

Carter stared at the empty sarcophagus. Perhaps Ptahmes was resurrected at the prescribed hour, making it so that the Ottleys could not find a mummy? He shook his head in denial. No, that was impossible; the sarcophagus was beneath the earth. There was no way for the ancient Egyptian priest's physical body to pass through solid lead, rock and dirt. Not to mention, even with Carter's admiration for ancient Egyptian engineering, he couldn't believe they had constructed an alarm clock that would wake someone up after two millennia of slumber.

There was still something strange about the immense sarcophagus before him. He stared at it, marveling at both its size and construction. It was made of lead—not common for an Egyptian tomb. He stepped up to it and ran his hand along the edge, his fingers grazing the roughness of chisel and saw marks. That meant the sarcophagus had to have been forced open, so it must have been hermetically sealed. Most ancient caskets were simply closed with a slab of rock resting on top.

Tilting his head to take in the coffin-shaped structure, he found himself wondering why. Why should imperishable treasures, gold, silver and precious stones be enclosed in lead? Why not in stone? If it had only been intended as a treasure chest, surely something simpler would have sufficed.

"Wait a minute," Carter said out loud. He stepped back to take in the coffin, then it hit him what was so unusual about it.

The sarcophagus was at least four feet tall, about twice the height of other ones he'd seen. He leaned over it and extended his arm into the hollow interior. Eighteen, maybe nineteen inches deep—certainly not more. He lightly tapped his index finger against his lips as he pondered why.

He took a sharp intake of breath when the possible reason occurred to him. Perhaps the height concealed a second chamber hidden underneath the hollow that contained the treasure. His foot lightly thudded against what he hoped was an empty space below the main cavity, but the sound it emitted was anything but; not completely hollow, but containing something unknown.

Carter carefully lowered the lamp into the sarcophagus and examined the bottom. Its smooth, unbroken surface gleamed. He let out a low "huh" as he stood up again and considered what the difference between the eighteen inches of visible space and four feet of total depth might mean. Was the lower area filled with lead? If so, why such uneconomic expenditure of what at the time was a valuable mineral? His brows drew together in confusion.

The puzzle interested him so much he decided it must be solved at any cost. Returning to the first chamber, he searched about, finally finding a fine-pointed and razor-sharp chisel. He set to work.

Hoisting himself into the sarcophagus, Carter chose a place and, using his bodyweight instead of a hammer, pressed the chisel into the lead. Bit by bit it pierced through the metal. An inch. Then an inch and a half. Suddenly it broke through, and he fell forward as the handle caught him. The mystery was solved. The lower section was hollow. He grinned as he steadied himself again and wiped away the sweat on his forehead.

A sharp but sweet smell filled the air, familiar yet foreign. It was like camphor and violets and lavender and oil of almonds all at once, yet none of them precisely. A strange mix of emotions swept over Carter that he could not make any sense of—memories from times past, or maybe thoughts of what the future would hold? Whatever it was, it was both powerful and confusing.

An inexplicable sensation of immense age filled him. It seemed unfathomable but something inside him was certain that he had been alive for thousands of years, or at least lived before, in a distant past that stretched back into the mists of time.

Swarms of flickering lights played across the chamber's walls and ceiling. Surrounding him were people—or shapes that suggested humans—whose voices reverberated in unison with an ancient chant. His knees seemed to sink into the trough as if it had transformed into rushing waters that surged from some unknown depths. Everywhere he looked, spectral figures emerged from within the darkness, and billowing clouds of incense washed over him, causing his senses to reel. The cavern swung around him with nauseous rapidity.

He realized that he was becoming mysteriously anesthetized by something released through the chisel hole, and he stuffed it closed with his handkerchief. With a powerful effort, he tumbled more than climbed out of the sarcophagus, ending up sprawled on the floor. Struggling to his feet, he staggered toward the fresh air.

He mechanically trudged to the temple entrance until his feet touched the sand outside, and he had to blink several times in surprise. About fifty paces away, a grove of palm trees suddenly rose out of the barren landscape. They weren't there before. Carter told himself that they couldn't be real... he was probably just imagining it all. It was a mirage.

The leafy fronds cast dappled shadows on the ground, but the cool air wafting from within the grove made his feet guide him forward. The oasis was an illusion, he knew—he knew it—but he still could not resist its call.

Carter entered the grove and followed a winding path to a little stream that ended in a pool, its water glittering in the sunlight as he knelt to dip his hands in its shallow depths. The moment he touched the liquid, a figure emerged from the pool—an ethereal nymph with long, black hair that shimmered in the light like a raven's wings. Her movements were languid and soothing as she stepped from the pond, streams of water tracing the curves of her body as they dripped, sparkling and glistening, to the ground.

She sat in the sand next to Carter, grasped his hands in her own before pressing a gentle kiss upon them. Removing his hat, she ran her fingers through his hair, singing a wordless melody so sweet and pure that it made time itself stand still. Her fingers slowly, button by button, opened his shirt. Transfixed by her beauty, Carter made a feeble gesture of protest before letting his hands drop to his sides. The nymph ran her hands up his chest, then slipped off his shirt.

It was most pleasant. With a contented sigh, he settled his head in the soft curve of her lap. As she sang, each note wrapped itself around his heart and soul. The melodies cradled him in a warm embrace, lulling him into a state of pure pleasure. Eventually, he could not resist the sweet lullaby any longer, and he released himself to the peaceful melody as his eyes fluttered closed.

CHAPTER FOUR

The nymph smiled and laughed, teasingly sprinkling drops of cold water over Carter's face and chest. He snorted like a pig and sat up, soaking wet. "That's cold!" he exclaimed.

The nymph, the palm tree grove and the pond evaporated in an instant. He snapped awake to find himself sitting up in a cot inside of a tent. For a confused moment, he glanced around and took in his surroundings; his shirt lay, folded neatly, on a nearby trunk, his solar topee perched on top. His holster coiled next to them, and his boots, lined up as though set out by a valet, rested on the ground. The sound of dripping water pulled his attention to the figure seated by the cot: Miss Ottley. She twisted a wet towel in her hands, squeezing out its contents into a metal bowl resting by her feet.

"The fact the water felt cold is actually good news," she said with the tone of an unsympathetic nurse. She tossed the cloth into a bowl, causing its contents to splash. "It's a sign that your body temperature is returning to normal." She placed the back of her hand against his forehead. "Your skin is no longer clammy, which is also a relief." She shook her head with an angry sigh. "I found you outside, not wearing your shirt or hat, sprawled out in the sand, clearly suffering from the beginnings of heat prostration." Her breathing was irritated as she continued speaking. "You have to respect the sun of the desert, Mr. Pinsent. You can't treat it as though you're on holiday at the seashore."

"I am very well aware of the dangers of the sun in Egypt, Miss Ottley." Carter matched her curt tone. "I've traveled here with my parents on various archaeological expeditions since I was ten." He flopped back onto the cot, placing one arm across his eyes. His head pounded. "It must have been the perfume's doing. That has to be it."

"Perfume? What perfume?"

Carter pulled his arm down. "From the sarcophagus. When you...'relieved' me to sit with your father, I went back into the temple. There is something odd about that sarcophagus. It kept bothering me, so I examined it closely. When I punctured the surface with a chisel—"

Miss Ottley stood, furious. "You did what? How could you have damaged the sarcophagus? How dare you!" She spun around with military precision and marched out of the tent.

"No! Wait! Don't go near the sarcophagus, it could be dangerous!" Carter sat up, then gripped the edge of the cot as a wave of dizziness swept him. Taking a deep breath, he grabbed his boots and hurriedly put them on, along with his hat. He sprinted out of the tent and stopped for a moment to let his eyes adjust to the glare.

Holding one hand above his eyes, he looked around, searching for Miss Ottley. She was entering the temple. "No! Don't!"

He sped after her, still groggy and weaving a little, arriving in the second chamber just as Miss Ottley was about to take his handkerchief out of the chisel hole. "Stop! What are you thinking? Don't be a fool!" Carter shouted as he ran over and pulled her hand away from it.

She yanked her wrist out of his grip. "Where do you get off calling me—"

"Will you just shut up and listen to me for a minute, please?" Carter fired back.

Miss Ottley sighed and lifted both hands in a gesture of resignation. "Fine."

"About the sarcophagus, let me explain." Carter placed the palms of his hand together as he gathered his thoughts, trying to ignore his headache. "The treasure filled this hollow area at the top, correct?"

"Yes."

"Why was it there?"

Miss Ottley crossed her arms. She sounded like she was speaking to the village idiot. "Tombs frequently held valuable objects, such as gold and jewels. You should know that."

"I do know that, thank you very much, and that is true for normal tombs. But I think this particular one is different, for two possible reasons." He paused. "Would you care to hear why?"

She gestured for him to continue, as if to say "why not."

Carter counted off on his fingers. "One, Ptahmes must have known about graverobbers. They've been around for ages, so perhaps the treasure was intended as a bribe, as it were, for thieves to take and not disturb his body scrounging around for more. The second possibility is based on his own prophecy. Ptahmes realized he would need some funds when—if—he woke up from his long nap. He couldn't just walk down to the corner bank and cash a check. Since the sarcophagus was sealed—as witness the marks of tools required to open it—that was probably the case."

Miss Ottley watched him intently. "Go on."

Carter stepped back and took in the entire sarcophagus with a sweeping gesture. "Now, consider this sarcophagus. It's just not right. The proportions are off, aren't they? The hollow part versus the whole thing. Height versus depth, I mean."

She looked over the sarcophagus and then nodded.

"So that leads to a question: what's in this bottom section, under where the treasure was? Listen." Carter tapped his foot against it. "It doesn't sound empty, but not entirely solid, either. Something is down there." He pointed to the chisel hole. "I punctured the lead to see if I could discover what the contents of the lower part were. When I did, I released a perfume... a gas, a mist. I managed to stuff my handkerchief into the hole to stop it, but I already had fallen under its influence. That's why you found me the way you did. The perfume must have a hallucinatory effect."

Miss Ottley didn't say anything, but regarded Carter thoughtfully.

"We know the ancient Egyptians used aromatics like cinnamon, cassia, cumin, anise and myrrh as part of their burial practices, as part of the mummification process and for odor control," he went on. "The perfume coming from that hole didn't smell anything like those spices, but its presence does suggest one thing."

"What is that?"

"The obvious conclusion is Ptahmes' mummy, or his body, or a body, may still be present." Carter again tapped the bottom of the sarcophagus with his toe. "The old boy is simply occupying the lower berth."

Miss Ottley stared at the sarcophagus, then shifted her gaze to Carter, for the first time looking at him as something other than a dimwitted servant. "Of course!" she whispered. "Brilliant!" She took his hand. "Come. We must tell my father."

Miss Ottley hurried toward her father's tent like a late passenger rushing for a train, with Carter in the role of the dawdling child being dragged along. Sir Robert was dozing when they went inside. Miss Ottley knelt beside the cot and gently woke him. "Father... Father..."

Sir Robert opened his eyes and gave a weak smile.

Miss Ottley gestured for Carter to come closer. "Father, Mr. Pinsent has expressed an interesting idea I think you should listen to." She stood and guided Carter to Sir Robert's side.

Carter told him of his experiment with the sarcophagus and his conclusions. Sir Robert listened with the most passionate attention. "You did not see Ptahmes?"

"No, sir."

"You are sure the sarcophagus does contain the body, though?" Sir Robert asked.

"I'm not completely certain, Sir Robert," Carter replied, "but I believe it is a strong hypothesis."

"Yet you told me earlier, if I remember correctly, that, that—"

Carter interrupted, "You were almost out of your mind from the fever at the time. I had to get you to relax, so I told you that it was likely your wish would come true. However, now I think there's a strong possibility a body is in the casket."

"As do I. The papyrus speaks of an essential oil the mere scent of which arrests decay. Ptahmes alone knew the secret of its preparation," murmured Sir Robert. After a second, he added, "Now, you must be careful of yourself."

"Careful?" Carter repeated, puzzled.

"Aye," Sir Robert mumbled, as though becoming more tired, "you may have incurred his wrath."

"What wrath? Are you talking about a curse?"

"Yes. The curse which Ptahmes directed against all those who desecrate his tomb," Sir Robert cautioned, "as he wrote in the papyrus."

Carter's mind flashed to the mysterious shadow he saw in the tomb for a moment and a chill ran down his spine, but he swatted the fear away. He grinned instead. "Come, come, presently I will be thinking you a superstitious man, Sir Robert."

"Do you believe in God?" he asked.

"Of course," Carter retorted.

"Then are you not superstitious, too?" Sir Robert enjoyed his question.

"If anybody bears the wrath of Ptahmes' so-called curse, it would be those who stole the treasure," Carter argued, more to convince himself than Sir Robert.

"You punctured the coffin, and disturbed his final resting place," Sir Robert said. "You may have triggered the curse unwittingly—but still you have incurred it nonetheless. But there, I have warned you. I'll say no more. I thank you for your insight regarding the sarcophagus."

He closed his eyes, evidently dropping off to sleep again. Miss Ottley tugged on Carter's arm, pulling him out of the tent. Outside, she gazed at him with a pleasant smile, almost like he was a friend.

"Now it is my turn to cook my specialty for you," she said. "Eggs and bacon?"

Crater returned the smile. "That would be most welcome. I'll get my shirt on."

Miss Ottley winked. "No need to do it on my account."

She rushed off to the cook tent, leaving Carter wondering if his cheeks matched his hair color. As he walked toward her tent, he couldn't help but wonder why Sir Robert's daughter had suddenly changed her demeanor towards him. Was it because of the information he had shared with her father, which could potentially be useful for their mission? Or perhaps she was finally starting to see him as more than a bumbling fool? Inside the tent, he put on his shirt and holster, his mind racing with questions and doubts, his confusion only amplified by his lack of understanding of women. Which probably explained his only handful of dates.

He sat in the shade of the temple. Glancing in the direction of the Nile, he noticed a column of moving smoke. A small steamer, no doubt, and what was more likely was that it should contain soldiers, Arabs, servants, and, most likely, a surgeon.

Miss Ottley came up to him with two plates of food. She handed one to him and sat down.

Carter pointed toward the smoke. "That must be your dragoman returning with a rescue party. They should be here very soon. I will soon be able to return to my dig, it seems!" He dove into his food, hungrier than he thought he was. "Excellent. Compliments to the chef."

She laughed. "Thank you. How can we ever repay you and your father, Mr. Pinsent, for your kindness to us?"

"Firstly, can we leave off the formality?" He leaned toward her and waved his fork around the general area. "We are not exactly surrounded by the polite tea and crumpets English society out here. Mr. Pinsent is my father. My name is Carter."

She relaxed her shoulders and smiled. "Agreed. You can call me May."

Carter bent his head to one side and studied her intently before repeating her name with a warm smile. "May."

She returned the smile. "Carter."

"Might I now make another request?"

"Of course."

"Allow my father and I to be present when the coffin of Ptahmes is opened." Carter popped a slice of bacon into his mouth. "It would be most interesting."

"I will ask my father to send for you as soon as he is well enough to investigate the coffin," May promised.

"Thank you. I look forward to it," Carter said.

"You said you came with your parents to Egypt before. Is your mother here as well?" May asked after a pause.

Carter's fork clinked against his plate as he absentmindedly moved the eggs around. "My mother passed away a year and a half ago. She was taken by a sudden illness." His voice cracked, and he cleared his throat before continuing. "I was at school when the telegram from my father arrived. Even though I took the next train to London, I didn't reach the hospital in time."

May touched his hand. "I'm so sorry."

Just then the party from the launch arrived at the camp, ending the conversation. It consisted of Sir Robert Ottley's dragoman, half a company of Egyptian camel corps under the command of a fussy little lieutenant, some twenty laborers and an Englishman.

The latter was a rather singular person. He was middle-aged, short and thick, with a full beard seemingly all the way up to his very eyes. It immediately appeared to Carter that the newcomer's ego made up for his lack of stature.

May's body became rigid as she got to her feet to welcome the new arrivals. Carter followed suit, standing with unease.

"Dr. Belleville, I am glad you have arrived!" May strode toward the short, bearded man.

"Your dragoman informed me of the incident, and—" Dr, Belleville suddenly noticed Carter's presence. "Who is this young man? Why is he present?"

"Mr. Pinsent and his father came to our assistance after the attack." May made a slight referential wave of the hand towards Carter.

Dr. Belleville narrowed his eyes at Carter, a thin line of disapproval etched on his furrowed brow. He gave a single curt nod, then grunted softly, the closest thing to appreciation he could manage, Carter supposed.

"Is your father still in the temple?" Dr. Belleville took a couple of steps toward the entrance, apparently certain of the response.

"No," May said. "He was moved to his tent."

Dr. Belleville immediately opened fire. "You should hardly have permitted movement of the patient for a day or two. He was probably in a very weakened state."

"The senior Mr. Pinsent made that decision," May responded. "I was unable to prevent it. I was removed from my father's side. By force." She cast a meaningful glance back at Carter.

"My father was doing what he believed was correct for the situation. He is not a doctor and it was an emergency," Carter responded angrily. He waited for some support from May. It didn't come. "Anyway, the thing is done."

"Take me to Sir Robert immediately," Dr. Belleville commanded with a flourish of one hand.

"Certainly. This way." May led the doctor toward the tent. Neither gave Carter a second glance.

Carter stood there, a mix of anger, confusion and frustration swirling inside him. He took a couple of angry steps after May, not being able to figure out the sudden transformation in her behavior. Was she the same person who had just shown him kindness and warmth, or was this cold and distant version the real her?

"That's gratitude for you," he forced out through gritted teeth. "The next time you find yourself in a bad situation, might I suggest you don't bother coming to us for help."

With an angry growl, he turned on his heel and found himself the object of stares from Sir Robert Ottley's dragoman, the half a company of Egyptian camel corps under the command of the fussy little lieutenant and the twenty laborers, all spectators of the little scene which had just unfolded. Carter was the lone actor stranded onstage when the curtain didn't fall, but he wasn't going to slink off to the wings. He stalked up to the soldiers.

Switching into Arabic, he informed the lieutenant about the robbery, where the thieves may have fled and suggested it would be a rather jolly good idea for his troops to pursue them. The little officer appeared pleased that somebody had at last given him something to do, so he puffed out his chest and barked orders to the corps. As they left, Carter spun on the dragoman.

"Your Arabic is excellent, sayyid." The man bowed slightly. "But I speak English. I am called Hassan Ali. What... suggestions do you have for my men?"

"Clean up the first chamber in the temple and post guards so an incident like this doesn't happen again," Carter shot back. "That would be a good start, don't you think? I'm sure Miss Ottley will have other instructions,"—he tossed a glare toward Sir Robert's tent—"once she is finished her consultation with the esteemed Dr. Belleville."

"It will be as you wish, sayyid." Hassan Ali bowed again. He added with a hint of a smirk on his face, "Will you be remaining here in camp?"

"No," Carter answered. He tapped two fingers to his hat in a salute. "Ma'a as-salāmah."

"Ilā al-liqā'," the dragoman replied with a knowing smile.

Carter hesitated a second, surprised that Hassan Ali had used a form of farewell which implied a future meeting. Dismissing it from his mind, Carter mounted his donkey with as much dignity as he could muster, then dragged the head of the animal to face his camp.

The beast, however, would hardly budge. Burning with embarrassment, he had to yell and kick at him unmercifully to induce forward movement. The mocking chuckles from the workers assured Carter that he looked completely ridiculous. At that point, Carter developed an ineradicable hatred of donkeys. Finally the creature decided to move, and he rode out of range of the laughter.

Once away from the camp, Carter told the desert exactly what he thought of Sir Robert Ottley, Dr. Belleville, Miss May Ottley and girls in general, and in no uncertain terms. He was so engaged in his rant that he almost completely missed his father riding in the opposite direction.

"Carter! Carter!" his father called out.

Carter reined in his donkey and waited until Mr. Pinsent rode up to him.

"Why are you going toward our camp?" Father asked.

"It seems our services are no longer necessary." The bitterness in Carter's voice was palpable. He told his father of the launch's arrival carrying Dr. Belleville and the others, and for a moment, the thought of May's dismissive treatment made him angry and embarrassed all over again. Yet he contained it, refusing to speak about it.

"Belleville?" Mr. Pinsent started. "Dr. William Belleville?"

"We were not formally introduced," Carter acidly responded. "He's a short man, with a full beard. Full of himself."

His father nodded. "That's William Belleville."

"It sounds like you know him."

"I'm acquainted with his reputation. He was barred from medical practice a few years ago due to the use of 'unorthodox' treatments," Mr. Pinsent said. "He is also a spiritualist."

Carter was incredulous. "You mean, he believes he can contact those who have died? Communicate with them?"

"Yes," Mr. Pinsent said. "He has a medium chap in London—Oscar Neitenstein is his name. He holds seances at least once a month, frequently with Belleville and Ottley attending as well."

"Sir Robert is a spook-hunter too?" Carter shrugged. "How do you know all this?"

His father's eyes met Carter's, then he shifted his gaze to the sun-bleached sands. "Because once I went to one of Neitenstein's seances. I wanted to talk to your mother." His jaw tightened and he slowly pulled on the reins of his donkey, turning it towards their camp. His shoulders slumped as he rode away.

As they made their way back, Carter couldn't shake off his confusion. His father, the most rational person he knew, had resorted to consulting a medium in hopes of one last conversation with his deceased wife. It both baffled and saddened Carter, as he had come to terms with his mother's passing... well, accepted it, at least. But his father seemed trapped in a state of unrelenting grief, unable to move forward or backward, drowning in anger at the unfairness of it all. Carter felt completely helpless, as stupid as the stubborn donkey he rode on, unable to provide any comfort or guidance.

CHAPTER FIVE

Carter's skin glistened with sweat under the relentless desert sun as he and his father returned to their daily routine at the dig site. They worked side by side, using delicate brushes and small tools to prod the sand gently to surrender the ancient, buried relics. Despite the heat and exhaustion, Carter was exhilarated each time they unearthed a new object. It was like diving into a long-lost world, piece by piece, and learning its secrets through each artifact. The weeks flew by in a blur of excitement as replacement workers joined them and new discoveries were made almost every day. Slowly but surely, the events of the Ottley site began to fade from his mind, pushed out by the thrill of the present discoveries.

It was late one afternoon when Carter pounded the keys of a portable typewriter, trying to finish transcribing his and his father's notes. He spent as much time untangling the ribbon and refitting the jammed keys as he did typing, but he was determined to get the job accomplished before the sun went down. With an annoyed growl, he again pushed a couple of keys back into their correct positions when he heard a voice from behind him.

"Excuse me, sayyid."

Carter spun around on the campstool. The Ottley's dragoman stood at the tent entrance.

"Many pardons. I do not mean to intrude, but I am instructed to give this to you, sayyid." Hassan Ali bowed and held out an envelope.

"Shukran." Carter took the envelope and glanced at it. In a firm, but feminine, hand "Mr. Pinsent" was written. He tried to hand the communication back to the dragoman. "This must be for my father. He is out at the dig."

Hassan Ali shook his head and smiled. "No mistake, sayyid. She told me to give this to the young one."

Carter looked at the envelope and shrugged. He repeated "shukran" as he opened it and removed the folded note inside. The text was brief: "Mr. Pinsent: You left your medical kit here. You may come and collect it. M."

He flipped the page over to see if anything was written on the back. It was blank. Carter fumed. This was a summons! Of all the nerve! He turned back toward the dragoman. "Kindly inform Miss—"

Hassan Ali was gone.

Carter swore under his breath. With a sigh, he stood and headed for the dig, note in hand. He found his father on his knees, brushing the sand off a partially exposed pot. "Father, Miss Ottley just sent over a... request..."—he didn't try to hide his opinion of the matter from his tone—"for us to retrieve our medical kit we left at their camp." He attempted to infuse the statement with enough *we really don't need to do this, do we* tone, hoping his father would say not to bother.

Mr. Pinsent didn't take his attention from the pot he was examining. "Good idea. We really should have that back since we're leaving in a week. Silly I didn't think of it before. Would you fetch it, please?"

"I need to finish transcribing our notes." Carter's voice bordered on a whine.

"I'm sure they can keep for a short time."

Carter opened his mouth to protest but realized it wouldn't do any good. Finally he snapped, "Right, fine."

He carefully placed an old, weathered saddle onto a donkey before setting out to the Ottley camp. The sun was slowly sinking below the horizon, but its crimson rays still beamed from the sky and cast a red hue across the sand. He was glad for the full moon that was rising, which would provide enough comforting light for his return later.

When Carter arrived at the Ottley dig site, he immediately got the feeling that something was off. The area was eerily quiet, with no signs of the workers who had arrived earlier. As he dismounted, he noticed two looming figures—guards—standing next to the temple entrance. The sun glinted off the rifles in their hands.

"Your medical kit is in here, Mr. Pinsent," Miss Ottley called to him from the entrance to her tent. "Thank you for responding so quickly."

"How could I turn down such a gracious written invitation?" Carter replied with unveiled sarcasm as he walked toward her.

"Your father is pining to open the tomb of Ptahmes, I suppose, Miss Ottley?"

"He has opened it," she answered as she opened the tent flap.

"Oh!" Carter exclaimed, then remembered her promise to him to allow him to witness the event. He scowled.

She looked at him with professional sympathy. "I am sorry. I know I told you that you and your father could be present, but they permitted no one to be around to assist them."

"They?" The two stepped inside the tent.

"My father and Dr. Belleville. It took place the day before yesterday in the cave temple. And the tomb is now closed again. I'm sure you noticed the guards." She spoke with the clipped efficiency of a guide herding tourists through a museum. She gestured toward the medical kit, sitting on the floor.

Irritated still, he picked it up, but felt duty-bound to ask the next question. "And how is Sir Robert?"

May lowered her voice. "Carter..."

"Oh? We're back to 'Carter' now, are we?" Carter snapped.

Her mask fell off. She glanced around as though afraid to be overheard. She continued softly, "My father has greatly changed. He seems to be quite physically strong, but he has aged notably, and he will hardly condescend to talk with any-one, even me. Moreover, the subject of Ptahmes is tabooed. The very name enrages him. Dr. Belleville has forbidden it to be mentioned in his hearing." She took his free hand in hers. "I'm in trouble. I am in need of your help, Carter."

Carter glanced at her hands and saw they were ashen, trembling ever so slightly. A pang of guilt settled in his stomach at the thought of his rudeness. He nodded toward the cot for her to sit, put down the medical kit and sat next to her.

Miss Ottley fixed her gaze on Carter, her eyes a mixture of sorrow and apprehension. "I'm afraid my father's mind has been affected by... something."

"Dr. Belleville is a medical man, May," Carter pointed out gently.

"Dr. William Belleville is a Fellow of the Royal College of Surgeons," May acknowledged, "as he will frequently remind you. He is critical to my father's work because of his many important connections here and in England. Indeed, he introduced Ptahmes to him. And he is a horrid little man."

Carter couldn't contain a chuckle at the description. May gave him a small smile before her features were overtaken by an expression of sadness and dread. She looked to the ground.

"I am afraid of him—my own father." Her fingers tightened around Carter's. It was a nice good little hand—small, yet firm and silky smooth, and possessed a strange electric quality. "I have a feeling that he hates me, that he wants to—to destroy me."

"Oh, surely not," Carter soothed. "The strain of the search, the robbery, the shooting..."

May shook her head. "It is more. I was bringing my father's cup of tea to his tent one night. I thought he was alone, but I could swear I heard him talking to somebody."

"Talking? To whom?" Carter asked. "What was he saying? Could you tell?"

"He was begging somebody to be patient. I waited outside for the visitor to leave, but nobody did. I peeked through the flaps. My father was alone. The only thing I thought I saw—or thought I saw for only for a second—was a shadow."

Carter's scalp tightened. "A what?"

"A shadow," she repeated. "It seemed to be in the shape of a man. It vanished."

"It must... it must have been a trick of the light," Carter said in what he hoped was a convincing manner.

"Yes, of course it was. But why was my father conversing with a shadow? Is that the mark of a well man?" May asked.

"He could have been talking to himself," Carter suggested, "as a way to keep up his will... his spirit." He instantly regretted the choice of words.

May reassured him with a pat on the hand and a small smile. "That's kind of you to say. But you're a kind person, much kinder than I."

"Nonsense. But what do you think is happening? You're not suggesting something supernatural is occurring, are you?" Carter tried to toss off the next question lightly. "You don't think Ptahmes' curse is in action?"

May shook her head. She became more resolute. "The temple. I think it must have something to do with the temple. With what's inside. You did mention that perfume had a strange effect on you."

"Perhaps that is what happened." Carter thought a moment. "But if that were so, Dr. Belleville would be affected as well. Is he?"

May sighed and shook her head. "No." She was quiet for a second. "Whatever it is, it is centered in the tomb. I must know what it is."

"You are then unaware what they discovered inside?"

"Completely. I attempted to find out, but with no luck. I was not allowed in."

"Why don't you demand to see inside? Or speak of your concerns to your father, or Dr. Belleville?"

"Don't you think I haven't attempted that already?" May reprimanded. She took a deep breath. "My concerns were dismissed and I'm not permitted inside of the temple. That is that. Dr. Belleville treated me like a child. He all but told me to run away and play and allow serious people to work. This is why I need your assistance. Please."

"My assistance?" Carter shrugged. "What can I do, if even you are refused entry?"

May spoke as if she were a conspirator. "Take the medical kit and make sure the guards see you leave. Once out of their sight, take a roundabout route to the hills behind the camp." She pointed in the direction. "My father, Dr. Belleville and Hassan Ali—the only others still in the camp besides the guards and I—will be getting some supper soon. When they do, I'll distract the guards with a story about possible bandits near the rocks. With them preoccupied with me, you can sneak into the temple and investigate it."

"To look for what?"

"I don't know. You've already shown off your keen observation skills when you found the clues about the sarcophagus, so now see if there is anything strange going on inside that temple."

"I am flattered by your faith in me, but—"

May's grip tightened, and she leaned toward him with imploring eyes. "Carter, please." Her voice was so soft it barely registered above the tent canvas rustling in a slight breeze.

Carter smiled. "All right, May, I will do it."

May returned the smile and stood. She spoke loudly. "There is your medical kit, Mr. Pinsent. Is it all in order?"

"Yes," Carter replied in an equally loud voice. "Everything is fine."

May held the tent flop open for Carter to leave. "I hope you and your father have a successful season at your dig."

Carter secured the kit to his donkey's saddle. "Thank you, Miss Ottley. We have made some interesting discoveries." He glanced in the direction of the guards. They were watching him as he climbed aboard his mount. "Goodbye."

May waved. "Goodbye. And thank you again for all your help after the robbery."

"You're welcome, I'm sure." Carter kicked at his donkey, and it plodded away from the camp, hooves pounding the sand. As soon as he was out of view of the guards, he reined in his mount and scanned the area. The Ottleys' donkeys stood staked to a length of rope in the shade between two large rocks. He rode up to them, dismounted and secured his donkey next to them. If his got it into its stupid head to bray, it would not be suspicious since it would be assumed to be one of those belonging to the camp.

Carter scrambled up the steep slope, not only trying to keep his footing on the slippery stones, but to remain quiet. Crouching low, he darted between the boulders, finally pressing himself against the warm rocks. He peeked over the top of one, noting the guards at the entrance of the temple. Sliding down to the ground, he waited. He was nervous, excited... he'd never done anything remotely like this before. His call to action didn't take long. May's voice, urgent and fearful, reached his ears. Carter looked again.

May stood in front of the guards, extended her arm and pointed frantically to the rocky outcropping opposite where Carter hid. Her frantic words were incomprehensible to him, but whatever story she gave them worked—they swiftly abandoned the entrance, trotting behind the young woman as she moved with surprising agility ahead of them.

Carter wound himself up, then raced across the open ground to the temple and leapt up the steps leading to the entrance. He paused for a moment, glancing around as he caught his breath, trying to see if he had been spotted before darting inside. His feet pounded against the rock floor as he sprinted down the shadowy corridor and into the first chamber.

It hadn't changed much, except now one table was covered with beakers, flasks and jars filled with oddly colored liquids. Alcohol burners glowed softly beneath them, giving off a faint smell of smoke. Placed on the floor by the table were three devices which resembled personal breathing apparatus. Carter stepped into the second chamber, lit by a single lantern hanging from the scaffolding over the pit. He stopped with a sharp intake of breath.

The heavy sarcophagus had been overturned and now rested in the center of the cavern. Lying on the flat, leaden surface of the bottom was stretched out, stiff and stark, the naked body of a tall, brown-skinned man. His skin glistened with oil and his muscles and sinews were taut like coiled springs. It had, however, an appearance of life—or rather, of suspended animation, because it did not show any movement. His mouth was tightly shut; his eyes were, however, open slightly. Carter took a step to examine the body more closely when a voice stopped him.

"Mr. Pinsent, I presume?"

Carter froze where he stood, startled by the sudden interruption. He whirled around to find Dr. Belleville and Sir Robert framed in the chamber's entrance. The doctor's arms were crossed, with a smug expression of satisfaction on his face, while Sir Robert appeared almost ghoulish in the dim light. A sickly sheen of yellow covered his skin and Carter thought he detected a hint of unease flickering through the man's eyes.

"Your medical kit is not in this location. So what brings you in here?" Dr. Belleville questioned.

"Curiosity about the contents of the sarcophagus," Carter calmly replied. He gestured toward the body. "But I didn't expect to find a dead Arab. One of the workers? I wonder what the authorities will think."

"The 'dead Arab' you refer to is the mortal remains of Ptahmes." Dr. Belleville choked back a laugh. Sir Robert smiled.

"What!" Carter turned to gaze at the corpse.

"I am not surprised at your mistake." Dr. Belleville moved next to Carter. "The body is in a nearly perfect state of preservation. It is not a mummy in any traditional sense of the expression. I cannot fully explain the circumstances of its preservation as of yet, but I can tell you this much now. We found it steeped in an essential oil which through a hermetic process had defied decomposition. However, the oil began to evaporate immediately when exposed to the air, but I managed to save a certain quantity with which, later, I purpose to analyze and experiment with in London.

"The Egyptian authorities you referred to have been very good to me. They have given me all necessary powers to deal with my discovery as I please. I only tell you that in case professional jealousy from you or your father should lead you to attempt any interference with our actions."

"Mr. Pinsent," said Sir Robert as he bookended Carter on his other side, "in a few days, Hassan Ali is setting out for Cairo. He will accompany Ptahmes and the sarcophagus on a truck to a launch, then to Cairo and journey to England. We will follow. If you promise to keep quiet about what you have seen today, I will deposit for you in a personal London bank account the sum of one thousand pounds."

Carter looked between the men. "In other words, Sir Robert, you wish me to understand that this finding is for you two only and not for the world."

"Oh, hardly that, my dear Mr. Pinsent, hardly that," Dr Belleville responded with a jovial smile. "It is we merely propose to choose our own time for taking the world into our confidence."

"An unusual course for a professed scientist to adopt, is it not?" Carter challenged.

"I have very little sympathy with conventionality," cooed Sir Robert.

"Nor I," added Dr. Belleville.

"The point of view of two burglars," Carter observed.

"You can be as rude as you please. You and your father saved my life," said Sir Robert.

Dr. Belleville cleared his throat. "The discourtesy of the disappointed is a tribute to the merits of the more successful, Sir Robert."

Carter glared at Dr. Belleville.

"Perhaps two thousand will ease that disappointment," said Sir Robert.

"And suppose, on the other hand—" Carter began.

"Oh!" Sir Robert gasped. "It is a simple matter of price. I should have known it! Make it three thousand, then!" Carter opened his mouth to reply, but Sir Robert spoke again. "Five thousand!" He broke into a wild, uncontrolled laugh.

Carter turned to ice. May could be right; perhaps her father was losing his grip on sanity. He spoke slowly and carefully to try and quiet the old man. "Let's take it easy, Sir Robert. There's no need for excitement. Let's all remain calm and remember this is merely a business arrangement."

Sir Robert suddenly stopped laughing, as though turned off by a switch. "Listen to me carefully, young man," he warned, his tone cold. "If you want to live another day and also not put your father's life at risk, then you'll stay out of our way."

"Is that a threat?" Carter said with disbelief.

"A threat, a bribe, call it what you will. I will transfer the funds into a bank account and send confirmation to your camp. You keep the money, consider this incident closed and we'll never cross paths again. That's all I'm willing to offer you. Do we have an agreement?" Carter found himself staring into the muzzle of a revolver. "Or not?"

Dr. Belleville purred in a velvet-like voice, "No need for violence, Sir Robert. Not yet, at least." He snapped his fingers. The two guards stepped into the dim chamber. "This can be a lawless area, Mr. Pinsent, and robberies can occur anywhere at any time, as Sir Robert unfortunately discovered. Your father and you could also find that out, although this time with fatal results. But not necessarily quick ones." He gestured to the larger of the two men. "Ahmed here has been known to take his enemies out into the desert and, one by one, bury them up to their necks in sand." He paused for a moment, before clasping his hands in front of him and adding softly, "An ugly way to die. Might I suggest you accept Sir Robert's kind offer of a thousand pounds for your... cooperation."

Carter glanced between the two men. "Given the situation, I suppose that is the most rational option."

Dr. Belleville's face creased into a malicious, triumphant smirk. "You are wise beyond your years, young man. But heed this warning: do not breathe a word of this to anyone—anyone at all. I have eyes everywhere. If you cross us, both you and your father will pay dearly for any indiscretions. You may even think yourself safe while you sleep, but my agents never rest. They are always watching, like shadows in every corner, in every room. They are of this world and the one beyond."

"The world beyond?" Carter attempted to push away his unease with a joke. "Are you talking about your spooks?"

Dr. Belleville gave a slight shrug. "If you insist upon calling them such. Who else am I referring to? Beware, Mr. Pinsent. They will not show you mercy in life or death should you defy me. Their tortures are far beyond human imagination, and they simply are waiting for my command. But until then, they are watching you. Always."

Sir Robert's eyes glittered like a maniac's as they peered across the sights of his revolver. "Go away!" he whispered.

Dr. Belleville made a sweeping gesture toward the entrance. The guards stepped aside. "You may leave now."

Carter turned to go.

"Do keep in mind, Mr. Pinsent," Dr. Belleville said, "silence is golden. And much healthier, as well."

Carter flushed with anger. He opened his mouth to tell Dr. William Belleville, F. R. C. S. and Sir Robert Ottley exactly what they could do with their money and Ptahmes, but their threats made him think better of that. He strode out of the chamber.

CHAPTER SIX

The memories of Sir Robert's maniacal laughter and Dr. Belleville's intimidation chased Carter as he stepped outside the temple. He stopped to try to make sense of what had just happened. He didn't believe he was a coward, but at that moment he couldn't deny the fear that coursed through him. The thought of being manipulated and controlled by those two filled him with a mixture of anger, dread... and helplessness. There was no doubt that Dr. Belleville would follow through with his threats.

What could he tell May? Nothing. How could he with the ultimatum Dr. Belleville slapped in front of him? He hated to violate the trust May had placed in him, but he had to... for his safety and his father's. All he wanted now was to put as much distance between himself and this insane place as possible. Without running into May.

The intense heat of the day had given way to a cool nighttime breeze, and the desert sand glowed eerily in the pale moonlight. As Carter hurried past May's tent on his way to his donkey, she rushed up to him and fell into step.

"Well?" she whispered. "What is happening in there? What did you see?"

Carter didn't break his stride and simply shook his head 'no'.

"The guards are watching us again. Is that why you can't answer?" May asked with a glance over her shoulder.

He didn't respond as the two rounded the rock outcropping and headed for the grazing donkeys. It was bad enough he couldn't give her any information, but not being able to tell her why made it worse. May grabbed him by one arm.

"We're out of sight of the temple. What did you see?" she said in a harsh whisper.

Carter yanked free of her grasp. "I can't tell you."

"What!"

"I can't tell you," he repeated firmly. His insides churned.

May sped up and blocked his path. She took hold of both his arms and stared into his eyes. "What do you mean by that?"

"Just what I say," Carter said. "I can't tell you anything. I'm... I'm sworn to secrecy."

"Sworn to secrecy?" May echoed in a stunned voice. "Sworn to secrecy! What sort of nonsense is that?"

"It's not nonsense." Carter broke free of her grip again. "It's the truth."

"Secrecy pledged to whom? My father? To Dr. Belleville? Why?" May demanded.

"I can't say. I'm sorry." His discomfort was growing into physical pain in his stomach. He stepped around her and continued toward his donkey. She pursued him.

"I got you inside that temple so you could see if anything in there is affecting my father, and now you return with this fairy story about being sworn to secrecy!" May hissed.

Carter spun around to face her. "It is not a fairy story. It's just that—"

"You promised—"

"I never promised anything!"

He stopped as Hassan Ali approached the two. As he passed, he bowed to the pair with a cautioning smile on his face. "Sayyid, permit me to help you with your ass."

"Thank you," Carter responded. He took a deep breath and faced May, and spoke loud enough that the dragoman could hear. "There is nothing unusual happening inside the temple. Nothing at all." He took the reins of his donkey from Hassan Ali and mounted it. "I'm sorry that I..." —he almost said 'let you down' —"...I didn't see anything of interest. Good night."

May's eyes bore into him, anger and disappointment warring on her face. Carter couldn't bring himself to meet her gaze any longer, not when he knew he had failed her. He jerked on his donkey's reins, urging the animal towards his camp. The thought of leaving her with no information made him sick with shame, but he had to think of his and his father's necks. There was no other choice for him than to retreat... a vanquished general surrendering the battlefield, abandoning the wounded to their fates.

Carter and his donkey plodded through the desert, its emptiness amplifying the thoughts churning through his brain. A breeze blew dust in his face, making his eyes sting. Only the occasional *plop-plop-plop* of the donkey's hooves on the sand broke the silence. Then, as if summoned by an unseen force, a piercing howl from a jackal echoed across the nearby dunes—an omen of disaster.

A sandstorm of emotions swirled around Carter, suffocating him—anger at Dr. Belleville's threats, anxiety about the worsening mental state of Sir Robert, guilt for failing May and lying to her. All topped off with his failure to stand up to them due t o... his cowardliness? Fear too, for his own future and that of his father... the possibility of being left an orphan. This all mixed in with puzzlement at the body he saw that Belleville claimed was Ptahmes yet was clearly not like any ancient mummies he had seen on Egyptian excavations in the past.

The donkey suddenly stopped, jerking Carter out of his thoughts.

"Come on, keep going, you bloody long-eared idiot!" Carter yelled, kicking his heels into the beast's sides. It refused to budge. "What's the matter with you now?"

With a loud, bellowing bray the donkey reared up and kicked its powerful rear legs again and again. Carter hung on desperately as he hurled curses and threats at the balking beast, but it was no use. With one last violent buck of its hind quarters, Carter went flying over the donkey's head, crashing into the desert sand with a bone-jarring thud. He lay there motionless, his face buried in the sand as the donkey ran off.

Carter sat up, spitting out grit, grumbling and swearing. He stopped, wondering if the donkey had spotted a cobra. Cautiously, he examined the area immediately around him for a sign of the hooded viper. The ground was empty.

Breathing a sigh of relief, his anger at the donkey's behavior returned. He stood, muttering as he brushed off his clothes. He turned and gasped.

A man stood roughly three feet away from him, mostly shrouded in black, like a silhouette in an unfinished painting. The only part illuminated by the moonlight was the face. It was one that sent shivers down Carter's spine.

The eyes rested large and dark beneath heavy brows, but were dull and lifeless, more like a corpse than a living being. The head tapered to a point at the chin. High cheekbones stood out against the shadowed skin of the countenance, making the long aquiline nose and thin lips stand out even more. The ears were pointed and laid flat along the skull like a bat's, and the chin was long and sharp with no hair.

Recovering from his first shock of surprise, Carter addressed the stranger. "What are you doing here? What do you want?" he cried.

No response came. Carter repeated the questions again in Arabic.

The figure remained silent.

"Answer me!" Carter ordered. "Ajb 'alayya!"

Carter clenched his fists as he recalled the events that had unfolded at the temple: the trouble with May and the business with that stupid donkey crashed into his mind. Now this silent stranger fired up the pent-up rage within him.

"I'll get an answer from you, one way or the other!" He stormed towards the figure and unleashed a right cross straight from the shoulder.

He struck air. The man had vanished.

The momentum from the punch carried him sideways for a few steps. Carter stood still, fists still doubled, confused. He turned a complete circle, scanning the desert.

The land was completely flat and empty; there were no dips or hollows in which the mysterious man could have concealed himself. He recalled the shadow he encountered in the temple, and Dr. Belleville's warning of having agents from "the world beyond".

Was something more at play? An existence beyond what his five senses could comprehend, a realm of spirits and supernatural beings? The mere thought sent chills down his spine. Was it possible that his reality and this other realm had somehow collided, or was it just his keyed-up emotions playing tricks on him? He prided himself on being a methodical thinker, relying on tangible evidence like pottery fragments and writings to draw his conclusions. Logically. Rationally. And he would do the same now—he rejected the idea of the supernatural.

"I must have been visited by one of Belleville's spooks!" His derisive laugh died on his lips as he looked down at the ground. His footprints were clear enough, but the sand was otherwise undisturbed. Any other markings were most likely disguised by a trick of the moonlight, he decided. He scooped up his hat and jammed it on his head. "Can't spend all night out here," he mumbled, and set off for camp.

It was after midnight when he reached his tent. The donkey was already there, calmly grazing on some hay. Carter resisted the urge to wallop the animal, but instead removed the medical kit and saddle before turning in for the night.

What was happening at the Ottley dig kept nagging at him. He kept those thoughts to himself though, because he and his father were returning to England at the end of the week and the preparations fully occupied his mind. They spent the remaining time bustling about the camp, cataloging artifacts and carefully packing them in crate after crate. Notes were filed, equipment stored. Carter now assumed that job he had seen his mother do many times in previous years, quickly and efficiently organizing the process.

He had just dispatched the last wagonload of relics bound for shipment on the steamer, checking the item off a list on his clipboard with a satisfied nod of the head, when he walked around the last remaining tents. On the other side, his father was reading a paper he held in his hand, fuming. Standing in front of him was a short man dressed in a crisp white linen suit despite the heat.

Carter stepped up to his father. "Is something wrong?"

"This! This is what's wrong!" Mr. Pinsent rattled the paper and slapped it with his free hand. "We've received a missive from the Department of Antiquities!" he roared at Carter. "They say there are problems with our paperwork. But our visas and permits are in order!" He turned toward the man, speaking louder and slower, as though doing so would solve the problem. "Our visas and permits are in order!"

The short man gave a helpless shrug, the type given by petty bureaucrats everywhere to indicate they were merely following orders. His smile, though, gave him away: he was enjoying the opportunity to display what little power he possessed.

Carter checked his watch and quickly formulated a plan. "Father, if you hurry you can catch the afternoon steamer to Cairo and deal with the Antiquities Department. There's not much left to do here, so I'll stay and finish up. Then I'll take a steamer to Port Said and wait for you at the dock."

"Exactly what I'd expect your mother to have said," Mr. Pinsent said softly. He folded the paper and slipped it into his pocket. "I'm off. I'll see you at the dock."

"Right. I'll be waiting," Carter grinned. "Good luck with the department. I'm anxious to hear how you deal with them."

His father left, still grumbling angrily under his breath about all this "bloody nonsense". Carter chuckled at his father's reaction, then looked at the official. He still wore that sanctimonious smile on his face.

"Do you require anything else?" Carter snapped at the man.

The man spread his arms and made a slight bow. He spoke with a thick French accent. "No, monsieur. My job is complete. Good day."

"Good day," Carter tartly responded. The man returned to his horse, a slight swagger in his step—the victor.

After his father left, Carter moved quickly to close down the camp. He dismantled the tent and piled supplies in neat stacks before handing out the final wages to the workers. Their voices faded as they left and the sun dipped below the horizon, and Carter stood alone in the sand, nothing but the donkey and his sleeping roll beside him.

Later that night, he sat by the fire cradling a cup of tea and gazed up at the stars, savoring their magnificent beauty. The fire cast flickering, shifting shadows on the sand. The warmth from the flames was a welcome change from the night air which carried an icy bite of the nights in that desert.

His imagination was wandering deep among the stars when a sound snapped him back to earth. He spun around to discover Ahmed standing behind him. In one smooth movement, Carter dropped his cup and rolled over to his blanket, swiftly pulling out his revolver and pointing it at the guard from the temple.

For a long moment, everything remained frozen. Then Ahmed moved his right arm. Carter cocked his gun. A smile spread across Ahmed's face as he held out an envelope.

Carter motioned to the ground with the revolver barrel. "Da'hu 'ala al-ard."

Ahmed knelt down and gently placed the envelope on the sand, another grin parting his lips. He rose up slowly, brushing the grains of sand off his hands, then backed away from the fire, dissolving into the shadows of the night until he vanished from sight.

Carter remained perfectly still, the firelight flickering across his face as he listened for any sound or other warning signs around him that Ahmed brought any friends along. After a few minutes of silence, he breathed out and eased the gun's hammer back into place. Still alert, he picked up the envelope.

He placed the gun next to him and tore open the envelope. It contained two sheets of paper. "Dear Mr. Pinsent," ran the letter on the first page. "Enclosed you will find the bank information for the account we discussed. Permit me to express a hope that you will uphold your portion of the agreement. Sincerely yours, Robert Ottley."

The second paper contained official bank confirmation of a "bearer" account from the Standard Chartered Bank with a balance of one thousand pounds.

Carter dropped the papers onto the sand with disgust. Accepting this money meant partnering with Dr. Belleville and Sir Robert on a scheme Carter opposed. But by not agreeing to their terms, he and his father could face possibly deadly consequences. Dr. Belleville and Sir Robert had enough power, influence and money to ensure such unpleasant repercussions occurred.

Carter stared at the documents, growing furious at his predicament. He wanted to fling them on the fire in an act of glorious defiance, but instead returned the papers to the envelope and slipped it into his hip pocket with a defeated sigh. He crawled into his bed roll, making sure the revolver rested close at hand.

He rose before the sun had even begun to light up the sky, readying his donkey for the start of a long journey. When he reached Méydûm, he quickly negotiated with a man at the market and soon enough, the donkey was sold for a low price—a bargain the man enjoyed as much as Carter was glad to be rid of the ornery beast.

Carter roamed around town, greeting the familiar faces and chatting with any former dig workers he encountered. Eventually he visited a small sidewalk cafe where he ordered an aromatic cup of coffee and some rolls. He made his way to the banks of the river by early afternoon and saw a waft of black smoke in the horizon—the steamer, miraculously arriving right on schedule. Once onboard, he discovered there weren't many other passengers on this trip. He obtained one of the cabins on the top deck of the two-deck ship.

The narrow ship hugged the bank as it churned its way to Port Said, the Nile cutting a mighty path past fields and villages. Carter leaned against the railing, taking in Egypt from the river, marveling at how little the land had changed in millennia. Farms lined both sides of the river, their crops waving gently in the breeze. Here was a field, the heads of the farmers bent over rows of vegetables; there, men coaxed dhow ships along the water.

A tug of hunger pulled at him as the sun descended behind the horizon in a blazing display. He went to the galley for a quick meal, then made his way to his cabin, just wide enough for two single bunks, stacked one over the other. The night was still oven hot, so he stripped off his shirt, boots and hat before sliding on top of the covers. After sleeping on cots and the ground for the summer, even the meager mattress of the bed was as welcome as a featherbed back at Buckingham Palace.

Carter's eyes flicked open suddenly out of a deep sleep, and he lay still, listening. The hair on his neck prickled with suspicion as he realized somebody else was in the cabin. He lunged upward, nearly barreling into the intruder—a figure hunched over him. The person darted away, and Carter scrambled out of the bunk.

He stepped onto the deck of the steamer and glimpsed a short man in a white suit quickly disappearing around corner toward the bow. Without hesitation, Carter took off running with long strides. It was a few hours past midnight, and there wasn't another soul in sight. The only sound came from the rhythmic wheezing of the smokestacks and the splashing of the ship's side paddle wheels.

Carter searched but couldn't find anyone, circling back to where he began. Then he realized what probably happened—whoever it was had disappeared into another cabin or down the stairwell to the lower deck, where he had plenty of places to hide. He swiftly made another round, this time keeping an even closer eye out, still finding nothing.

Giving up the search, he trudged to his cabin. His clothes were strewn all over the floor, obviously searched. He felt around in his pants pockets, and thankfully discovered he still had his wallet and the letter from Ottley. It seemed his visitor attempted to pickpocket him while he was asleep. Well, at least it was different taking place here than on the streets of Cairo.

Stretching out on his bunk, he linked his hands behind his head and drifted off again, waking up at the steamer's whistle sounding as it docked. He dressed and immediately visited the P. & O. steamship company offices. The man behind the counter, a tall, regal Englishman with silver hair, bushy eyebrows and a great mustache, nodded at Carter's name.

"Yes, Mr. Pinsent, your crates have been stowed on board the SS Persia, and your luggage is in your cabin," he said after flipping through a sheaf of papers. "Boarding time is 4:30 pm, Dock 7.

Oh, yes, this wire came for you." He reached into a rack of slots, extracted a telegram and handed it to Carter.

"Thank you." Carter took it and stepped away from the counter. Opening the envelope, he pulled out the yellow half-sheet of paper and read the message from his father: "Taking longer than expected. Will take later sailing. Meet you at home."

Carter tucked the telegram into his coat pocket. He felt a pang of sorrow for his father—as well as the Department of Antiquities staff if the Pinsent anger he and his father shared was unleashed. Glancing at his watch, he noted he had two hours to kill before boarding. He headed for Prince Farouk Street, stopping for a bite to eat at the Casino Palace Hotel, a sprawling, castle-like building complete with towers.

After his meal, Carter navigated his way back toward the port. As he negotiated the crowded streets, he couldn't shake the feeling that he was being followed, that his every move was echoed by an unknown presence behind him. He stopped for a moment to take in a shop window and moved so he could use the reflection in the glass to check behind him. It revealed a short man dressed in a white linen suit remaining motionless despite the surging crowd around him, his eyes focused on Carter.

Carter set off again, his pace quickening. When a group of British tourists momentarily came between him and his follower, he quickly veered into an alley and flattened himself against a grimy brick wall. His heart pounded as he waited for the man to pass. When he did, Carter sprang from his hiding place and bolted after him. Grabbing the man by the shoulder, he spun him around so they stood face-to-face.

"You're not," Carter asked calmly, "following me by any chance, are you?"

The man from the Antiquities Department put on one of his smiles with the same ease as pulling a clean pair of socks out of the dresser. "I assure you, monsieur, I am not following you. I simply needed to catch up with you. You are young and walk too fast for one of my age."

"Now that you've caught me, what do you want?" Carter crossed his arms.

"Merely to do my duty."

If ever a weasel could ever take human form, it stood in front of Carter now. "Which is?"

"Regrettably, I must inform you of a problem with your shipment of artifacts," the man said with an expert display of faked sincerity. "You must report to the inspector at the P. & O. shipping shed immediately, or your items will be put off the boat."

Carter exhaled an irritated breath.

The man spread his arms and made a slight bow. "My job is complete. Good day."

"By the way," Carter said. "How did you enjoy the steamer journey down the Nile?"

The man looked back at Carter. Again came the smile. "Steamer? You must be mistaken. I came here on the train." He bowed again and melded with the crowd.

Carter glanced at his wristwatch and swore under his breath. He took off at a sprint, dodging pedestrians on the busy street, finally reaching a brick warehouse. He stepped inside through the fifteen-foot-wide doorway and took a few minutes to catch his breath.

Boxes, crates and trunks of all sizes filled the large building, crisscrossed with aisles, forming an elaborate maze. He decided the inspector's office was probably located on the far side. His footsteps echoed on the concrete floor as he walked past row after row of cargo. Halfway across, he stopped at an intersection to get his bearings. Two workers were bent over a large crate nearby, discussing something. They would know where the inspector's office was located. He walked up to them and cleared his throat.

They lunged at Carter, one clamping an iron grip over his mouth while wrenching his arm viciously behind him. With lightning speed, the other brandished a syringe and stabbed it into Carter's arm. Carter struggled in their grip before his body jolted for a moment. He went limp and crumbled to the ground.

CHAPTER SEVEN

Carter's eyes fluttered open, and he took a deep breath. Instead of fresh air, he drew in a musty, stale scent that almost made him gag.

He tried to sit up, but his head smacked into something hard. Reaching up to touch what he had struck, his fingers rubbed against a slick fabric, silk or satin maybe, tacked to a hard surface.

Confused, he tried to take in his surroundings. Everything was completely black. He stretched out his arms and could barely move them. He lay in a confined space, only slightly larger than his body.

He reached around again, feeling for anything that could give him a clue as to where he was, but there was nothing other than the soft cloth. Then with a horrifying start, he understood where he was: inside a casket.

The reality of the situation crashed down around him. His chest seemed clamped as if in a vice, tightening as his heart pounded in his ears. Sweat started to bead on his forehead, and he gasped for air as a wave of dizziness came over him.

Carter closed his eyes and forced himself to calm down. He had to think rationally, systematically. What happened? How did he get here?

The last thing he recalled was standing in the P. & O. Line shipping shed in Port Said. Two workers jabbed him with a hypodermic needle, obviously filled with some type of sedative. Then he must have been dumped in this coffin.

And buried alive?

His breath caught in his throat as the terrifying thought crossed his mind. A wave of fear began to wash over him. He could almost see the cold dirt pressing down on the lid, worms wriggling toward their meal. Again he made himself get under control. Panic wouldn't help now. He must think, calmly.

He became aware of a gentle swaying, as if being rocked side to side. The sound of water sloshing against something, and a dull throbbing, as though the rumbling of engines, came to his ears. Understanding dawned on him: he was onboard a ship.

The coffin must be in transit, and Carter had been substituted for the original occupant. So, he reasoned, he must be in a ship's cargo hold. He hoped that the crew hadn't piled more boxes on top of the coffin in deference to its supposed contents. Time to try out that little hypothesis. Carter placed his hands against the lid.

He prepared himself mentally in case the top didn't budge. He pushed up.

There was a crack, followed by a gust of fresh air as he managed to lift the lid of the satin-lined oblong box. With a final heave, he wrenched the coffin open, the canvas covering it whispering as it slid to the deck. He sat up, relief flooding his body, and took in his surroundings in the dimly lit cargo area.

The casket sat by itself against one wall. In the center of the hold, four large packing cases made up a rectangular pile, almost filling up the entire space. Each box had been tightly tied down with rope and secured through steel ring bolts, their tops nearly reaching the ceiling. Smaller crates stacked together like a child's game of building blocks, held in place with crossed wooden beams, filled the starboard side of the area.

Climbing out of the coffin, Carter stumbled a few steps and braced himself against one of the large crates, the aftereffects of the sedative and the rolling of the ship making it difficult to keep his balance. He took in a few deep breaths and stood upright, trying to figure out how to get out of the hold or get in touch with a member of the crew. He didn't have to wait long. A gruff voice came from behind him.

"Looks what we have 'ere, Alfie."

Carter spun around to face two burly sailors.

"Somebody's come back from the dead, I thinks," one sailor said.

"Or 'es a stowaway," the second added. He shook his head. "Cap'n won't like that."

Carter stood by the desk in the captain's cabin. The skipper was large, with a full salt-and-pepper beard, leaning back in his chair.

By his side stood a slim, younger man sporting a neatly trimmed black beard, an officer's cap and an air of efficiency.

"I am not a stowaway." Carter had lost count of how many times he'd said that.

"And I remind you once more that you are aboard this ship without the consent of the shipowner or any other responsible person and were detected on board the vessel after departure. That is the definition of the term, and it makes you one," the captain said.

"Look, I've told you before," Carter tried one more time, his voice tinged with frustration. "I was booked on the SS Persia to London, and was lured into the P. & O. shipping shed..."

"Whereupon you were drugged, robbed of your watch, wallet and a bearer document for a thousand-pound bank account. Yes, yes, so you have said." The captain waved off the story. "It is obvious you are not Mister..."—he checked a sheaf of papers on his desk—"...Mister Roderick Manheim, late of Manchester, but you used his means of getting on board. By the way, where is Mr. Manheim now?"

"I don't know. Probably behind some crate at the P. & O. shipping shed," Carter said in exasperation.

The captain gave a groan of irritation, leaned forward and jabbed a finger at Carter. "What I would like to do with you, young man, and with all stowaways, is string you up, and lay fifty strong lashes across your bare back with a cat o' nine tails. Serve as a lesson." He spread his hands as he sat back and gave a regretful sigh. "But we live in the twentieth century, and do not perform such barbaric acts any longer." He turned to the officer. "But he tells one of the more creative stories I've heard, Mr. Jenkins."

"Aye, Captain," the first officer replied.

"It's not a story, it's true!" Carter yelled. "For the hundredth time, I'm not a stowaway! Why don't you listen to me? Are you deaf or merely stupid?"

The officer next to the captain shot Carter a warning look.

Carter picked up on it and continued in a calmer voice. "Sorry. Perhaps I've been upset. My father will pay for my passage once we arrive in London."

"This ship is not set up as a passenger vessel, nor do I intend to give you the opportunity for a free voyage if this father of yours doesn't exist," the captain shot back. He silently appraised Carter for a moment. "However, I do admire your persistence. Mr. Jenkins, are we at a full crew complement?"

Jenkins shook his head. "No, sir. Otis, one of the stokers, took sick in Cairo."

The captain looked back at Carter and folded his hands across his belly. "To show you I am a reasonable man..."

Anger flared in Carter. He opened his mouth to say something. Another warning glance from Jenkins shut it.

"I will offer you a choice," the captain continued. "I should turn you over to the authorities at our next port, as the shipping line requires me to do. However, from what I have heard, you would prefer the flogging to their treatment of criminals..."

"Criminal!" Carter bristled. A slight shake of the head from Jenkins silenced any further outburst.

"Or you can work off your passage to London by taking Otis' position in the boiler room, shoveling coal into the boiler. There you have it. I will abide by your decision. Which will it be?" The captain cocked his head to one side as he waited for an answer. He grinned. The silence was broken by the chime of the wall clock, shaped like a ship's wheel, an oddly delicate sound for the surroundings.

What choice do I have? Carter thought. He stood tall. "You have a new stoker."

"A most prudent selection. What is your name for the crew roster?" the captain asked.

"Pinsent. Carter Pinsent."

The captain repeated the name under his breath as he wrote it down on a piece of paper. He returned his attention to Carter. "All right, Pinsent, Mr. Jenkins here will take charge of you now and show you the ropes."

Carter curtly nodded. A silent order came from Jenkins' gaze with a tilt of his head toward the captain. Carter followed it. "Yes, sir. Thank you, sir."

"Dismissed." The captain turned back to his desk. The first mate led Carter from the cabin and down a passageway.

"He's not a bad sort, the captain," Jenkins commented with a jerk of his thumb back at the cabin.

"He certainly hides it well," Carter grumbled.

"It's just a stowaway started a fire on his previous command. Almost sank the ship." Jenkins stopped in front of a door. "In here."

They stepped into a storage room. The first officer rummaged through the ship's stores, finally producing a pair of pants and shoes. He put them on a counter.

"These should fit. This is all you'll want to wear in the heat of the boiler room, believe you me. Change into these and I'll stow what you're wearing in my cabin while we're at sea. At least you'll look presentable when we dock in London," he said.

"Thanks." Carter changed, handing his clothes to Jenkins. "By the way, what is the name of this vessel? I didn't have a chance to notice the way I came aboard."

Jenkins chuckled. "The Star of the Mediterranean. She's a good ship. Now I'll show you where you'll bunk, then I'll take you down to the boiler room. It will be your own little slice of hell, lad."

He was right. The sweltering heat in the boiler room was unbearable, a physical presence squeezing the life out of Carter like being wrapped in the coils of a python. He was standing in the core of a blazing firestorm, with flames devouring his body from every angle. The deafening roar of the furnace swamped his senses and his lungs choked with its soot-filled air, making him gasp for breath.

Hour after hour, day after day, week after week, Carter toiled, his muscles straining with the effort, a constant ache that threatened to overwhelm him with each move of the shovel. Stripped to the waist in a futile attempt to find any relief from the heat, sweat poured down his back, soaking through his trousers, ran down his face and stung his eyes, but his mind was focused on one thing.

Every shovel full of coal was a victory against those that had put him there and moved him that much closer to home.

After Carter showed he was willing and able to do the hard work of a stoker—indeed, he figured the more coal he shoveled into the boiler, the faster the ship would reach England—the crew adopted him as one of their own. He listened attentively to their stories and experiences from their time at sea, sometimes completely swallowing their tall tales, much to their amusement. They invited him to join their games of dominoes and dice, which Carter did with relish, as well as turning into a decent player of poker and euchre. The crew even bestowed a nickname he would carry proudly for the rest of his life: "Stowie."

Carter stood on the deck one glorious afternoon on a break from the hot boiler room, his muscles aching and sweat evaporating from his body. He relished escaping the stifling heat to take in the refreshing salty air. Grasping onto the cool metal railing, he gazed out at the vast expanse of rolling waves that stretched out before him. The vibrant blue ocean sparkled and glimmered, its rhythmic movement soothing and exhilarating. It is very different standing here from wearing a suit, sitting in a stuffy classroom while listening to a schoolmaster drone on. And the difference was becoming very appealing. Mr. Jenkins joined him at the rail and also looked over the sea.

"She seeps into your blood and works her way into your very soul, the sea does," Mr. Jenkins said softly.

Carter nodded. "I can see why. The adventure, not knowing what is beyond the horizon. The freedom."

"Aye, but you have to treat the ocean with respect, you do. She can be fickle and dangerous." The first mate remained quiet for a moment before turning to Carter. "Well, Stowie, it's been seven weeks. And I must say, you've turned into a right respectable member of the crew."

"Thank you, sir."

"Even the captain has said so."

"He has?"

"That he did. That's why he offered you that promotion to the bridge. You may not have changed his opinion of stowaways, but you've moved the needle a bit. We dock in London tomorrow," Mr. Jenkins went on. "Are you looking forward to it?"

"Yes, sir." Carter grinned. "I wonder if my father will recognize me."

Mr. Jenkins laughed. "I'm sure he will, lad, I'm sure he will. I'll return the clothes you, shall we say, 'boarded with' after we dock."

"Thank you, sir."

The *Star of the Mediterranean* tied up at a dock in London in the late afternoon. Down in the crew quarters, Carter tugged awkwardly at his shirt collar as he finished dressing. True to his word, Jenkins had returned Carter's old clothes, but it had been so long since he'd worn them they felt odd and constricting. He tucked in his shirt and made his way up on deck. The crew stood waiting when he emerged through the hatch.

"Alfie! Looks 'ere at this toff! Where'd he come from?" one yelled out.

"Now ain't 'e the cock of the walk!" Alfie called back.

"A regul'r Cupid's Swell, our Stowie is!" added a third,

Carter grinned. He showed off, turning around in a circle. "Behold, gents! This is what a sparkler looks like!" That prompted a chorus of hoots and cat calls.

Carter went up to the crew members, shaking hands, bantering and saying farewell. He would miss their camaraderie. Mr. Jenkins joined the group.

"Hop to it, lads!" the first mate bellowed in good-natured anger. "This tub isn't goin' to sail itself to Belfast!"

"Fair winds and following seas!" Carter called out with a final wave as the crew dispersed to return to their duties. He turned to Mr. Jenkins and shook his hand. "Thank you for all your help."

"Aye, lad, aye," Mr. Jenkins replied with a smile. "Best of luck to you. Just stay out of coffins from now on."

Carter laughed. "I plan to!" He headed for the gangplank and stopped, slightly surprised to see the captain standing there, even though he had warmed up to Carter over the weeks.

"Well, seaman Pinsent," the captain said, "are you sure you won't stay on for the rest of the voyage? Did you consider that promotion? This ship could always use a good man like you on the bridge."

"Thanks, Captain, I truly appreciate the offer. It would be a lie if I said I didn't consider it. But I'm home now," Carter said.

"I'm disappointed to hear that. Your passage has been more than paid." The captain stuck out his hand. "Best of luck, Stowie."

Carter grinned at the title and shook hands. "Thank you, sir." He saluted, the captain returning one of his own.

He walked down the gangplank to the dock and cast a surprisingly nostalgic final glance back at the Star of the Mediterranean. While he may have been back in London, he didn't have any money. That meant he couldn't take the Underground to Marble Arch, the closest station to his home, so a walk of a couple of hours lay in front of him.

"Best be off," he said to himself, and set on his journey.

The sun had just dipped below the horizon, casting an orange-pink hue over his street by the time he reached home and slowly climbed the front steps. Reaching for the brass handle, he opened the shiny black door and stepped into the familiar and comfortable hallway.

"Hello? Who is it? Who's there?" After a second, his father appeared in the open front parlor doors, holding the evening newspaper in one hand. At the sight of Carter, the paper fluttered to the ground and a torrent of words gushed out. "Carter! My son! Thank God! You're back! What happened? Where have you been? Are you all right?"

The two embraced. When they separated, Mr. Pinsent kept a grip on Carter's shoulders. "I've been contacting the Foreign Office every day, trying to get them to locate you." His eyes brimmed with tears. "If I had lost you, after losing your mother, I don't know what I would have done."

"Fortunately, you don't have to discover that, Father, as that calamity did not occur." Carter smiled. "Here I am in the slightly tired flesh."

"I expected to meet you here," Mr. Pinsent stepped back, examining Carter with a questioning gaze. "What on earth happened? Where have you been?"

Carter chuckled. "I've spent the last seven weeks in the boiler room of a freighter." He held up a hand to stop the next question. "But before I tell you of my adventure, I have a request."

"Yes?"

"This might sound strange, but more than anything right now, I want to take a hot bath."

"A bath?"

Carter laughed at his father's puzzled reaction. "The reason will become clear when I tell you my history."

"By all means." Mr. Pinsent gestured toward the stairs.

"I'll try to be down in a jiffy, although I warn you, it may be a long soak," Carter replied as he headed toward the staircase.

He entered the bathroom just at the top of the stairs, where he adjusted the taps until the water ran delightfully hot, steam rising into the room. After dropping in a drain plug, he peeled off his clothes and tossed them carelessly over a nearby chair.

Carter caught a glimpse of himself in the mirror. Shoveling coal for ten or more hours a day for a month and a half certainly had transformed him. His hands were calloused from the labor, the lines of his palms and fingers hardened. Not an ounce of fat remained on his frame, and lean, taut muscle packed his upper body and arms. Spending all his free time on deck had given him a deep tan. He grinned. The lads at school would certainly be jealous of him this coming term.

He slipped into the bath with a contented sigh. Just as he thought would happen, the infernal coal dust which seemingly had invaded every pore of his body rose, muddying the water into a murky gray. Closing his eyes, he completely relaxed.

A slight crash, as though something had fallen downstairs, caused him to open his eyes. "Father? Is everything alright?" he called out. He waited, but heard nothing else. His father must have dropped something. He shut his eyes again.

A scent, a sharp yet oddly sweet odor, wafted through the air. Instantly he sat up in the bath, anxious, trying to place the smell, shivering despite the warm bathwater dripping down his skin. His every muscle tensed when he recognized the aroma.

It was the perfume from the sarcophagus.

The doorknob rattled, then slowly turned until finally the door swung open. Standing, framed in the doorway, was the shadowy figure he'd seen before in the temple, flickering and rippling like a reflection in a pool of ink. Carter sucked in a breath. The shadow moved toward Carter—walking, floating, flowing—its movement unlike anything he'd ever seen.

"You're an illusion," Carter commanded out loud as the shadow reached the tub. "You're not real! You're just an illusion!"

The illusion grabbed Carter by the shoulders and shoved his head under the murky water. His body convulsed and thrashed wildly, flailing for air as the bathtub water sloshed over its edges. Carter's legs broke through the surface, kicking and twisting. Desperate for escape, he clung to the thing's arms, trying to pull them off. Bubbles streamed from his mouth. With a sudden surge of strength, he violently twisted free.

Carter sprung to his feet and lunged at the figure, grasping at the presence. As his fingers tangled with its form, he felt substance. Whatever this thing was, it was not a mere shadow, like he witnessed before. It had physical form, it had mass. It was a man.

The intruder clamped his hands around Carter's throat, choking him while pulling him out of the tub and shoving him into the corner with crushing force. With one hand Carter searched blindly for the shadow's face, his fingers brushing against what felt like a mask. He reached for where the chin should be. When he found it, he dug deep and exerted pressure, forcing the head back. A gasp of air escaped his lungs as the grip on his throat lessened. His other hand reached around and grabbed onto the intruder's hair. He yanked hard while simultaneously driving his knee into the stomach with devastating power. The grip around his throat was released.

Carter hurled himself at the shadow's waist, pushing them both through the open doorway and into the opposite wall. A picture dislodged at the impact, crashing to the floor. The two tumbled to the ground in a heap of flailing limbs, grappling as they rolled over and over. The shadow ended up on top, clamped both hands onto Carter's hair and slammed his skull into the boards.

His vision blurred, stars exploding in his eyes. In a final burst of energy, he summoned all his strength and swung his arm, landing solid punches on the side of the intruder's head. The shadow rolled off him.

Carter heaved himself up. He stumbled backward down the hallway a few steps until he bumped against a narrow table. As his attacker rose to its feet, Carter clenched the edge of the table and yanked it towards him. With a guttural roar, he rushed forward like a crazed bull, slamming his makeshift weapon into the shadowy figure's stomach like a battering ram with all his might and fury. The table splintered. The assailant was thrown off balance and tumbled down the stairs. Carter collapsed to the floor, dripping water and gasping for breath.

The muffled sound of footsteps on the wooden floorboards and a faint creak of the door came from below, followed by an unnerving quiet. Carter slowly sat up and shook his head to clear from it the last tendrils of the perfume. Using the railing for balance, he pulled himself into a standing position. He peered over the edge of the landing and saw an empty hall with the front door hanging slightly open. His assailant had fled.

"Father?" he called. There was no response. "Father? Are you all right?"

Carter slowly and cautiously went down the stairs, one wet hand gripping the railing. The usually normal ticking of the clock in the hallway sliced the ominous seconds into heartbeats, increasing the deep sense of dread cloaked around him. He inched all the way downstairs to the front hall. His gaze fell on the open parlor doors, and he went to them. Taking a deep breath, Carter crossed the threshold and peered inside. "Father!"

His father lay on his back, sprawled on the floor, looking like a broken doll left by a careless child.

CHAPTER EIGHT

The doctor extracted the syringe from Carter's arm and transferred the blood into a small vial.

"Do you think that will help, doctor?" Carter asked as he rolled down his sleeve. "Will it assist in my father's recovery?"

"I plan to assess the number of your red blood cells, white blood cells, platelets, the presence of parasites, unusual cell shapes and blood chemistry then compare that against your father's," the doctor replied. "It may give us more insight into diagnosis and treatment."

"You didn't answer my question," Carter said softly.

The doctor faced Carter. "There's always hope, Mr. Pinsent." He sighed and sat. "Your father's condition is a complete mystery to us. Despite your report of the attack in your home, there are no signs of any trauma on his body."

"He's in a coma, isn't he?"

"A 'coma-like state' is the best way to describe it, but it is not completely accurate," the doctor said. "He breathes softly but unmistakably. The heart rate has dropped to the point where it is difficult to detect a pulse. Blood pressure has been greatly reduced. Your father's body temperature has become cool. He is certainly unconscious, with no reflexes or reaction to external stimuli. His symptoms present more like some form of suspended animation, but as to what caused it..." He shrugged.

"It's not something like sleeping sickness, then."

The doctor shook his head. "However, you both recently spent time in Egypt, and it may be an illness that we aren't familiar with as of yet. Comparing blood samples may help."

"But if it is a case of some unknown disease, why haven't I come down with it?" Carter asked. "I was there at the same time."

"That is a very good question, Mr. Pinsent, for which I do not have an answer," the doctor responded. "You are in an excellent physical condition and show no symptoms whatsoever. Currently, there is one other patient in this hospital with the same condition as your father. They are the only two cases known."

Carter sat up straight. "Another patient? Who?"

The doctor flashed an apologetic smile. "I'm sorry. I'm afraid I can't give you that information."

"Of course you can't. Sorry," Carter said. "Can I see my father now?"

"Again, I must say no," the doctor said. "Not knowing if he has a transmittable disease or not, he must be kept in isolation."

"I see," Carter said. "So without a firm diagnosis, what can be done now?"

"We can administer intravenous fluid to maintain hydration, but the question of providing nourishment is a different matter," the doctor said. "While there has been some experimentation with external feeding tubes, the work has been performed only on animals and with mixed results."

After a few false starts, Carter finally managed to choke out the grueling sentence as the implications of what the doctor said set in, his voice heavy and thick. "So, if no one can accurately diagnose my father and provide him the right treatment, he will die from starvation."

"I'm sorry to say that may be the outcome, Mr. Pinsent."

Carter's body went limp as he slumped back into the chair. For a moment, there was complete silence. Finally, he coaxed the words out of his mouth, unwilling, fearful: "How long... how long does he have left?"

"Perhaps three weeks if there is no improvement in his condition."

Carter's eyes stung and shock threatened to overwhelm him. He tried to stay strong even though he wanted to break down right there in the examination room. Getting to his feet unsteadily, he barely managed a whispered "thank you" and "goodbye" to the doctor before bolting out of the door into the corridor, numb.

Tears welled up as he navigated the blurry hospital hallway toward the street. He took a deep breath to steel himself, his mind making calculations against his will. Three days had passed since the incident at his house. That left eighteen days. He had only eighteen days to do something, anything, to try to save his father's life. But what action could he possibly take? He left Saint

Bartholomew's, wiped his eyes then walked toward the Post Office tube station.

Questions still surrounded the events of that evening in Carter's mind, so perhaps beginning with what happened at his house and attempting to make the occurrence as clear as possible might provide a clue, or at least a potential direction. He recalled how the police inspector's eyes barely contained his disbelief when Carter explained he was attacked in his bathtub by a shadow figure. But, as unbelievable as it sounded, that is exactly what happened. So what was the reason? Why?

Could it have been Ptahmes' curse, as Sir Robert warned? Carter did smell the strange perfume from the sarcophagus just before encountering the dark intruder. But if the curse was the cause, why would the figure wait until just a few days ago to strike instead of doing so earlier? Why not appear on the deck of the Star of the Mediterranean and simply shove Carter over the railing? Wouldn't that have been easier?

Then Carter remembered that Sir Robert and Dr. Belleville brought the mummy to London. Maybe it had something to do with physical distance...

He shook his head. That didn't make sense, either. If a curse could travel across the unfathomable span of millennia, surely it would not be slowed by having to navigate a few miles through the city. Not to mention that the sight of a thousands-year-old mummy shambling down the lane would most certainly have drawn attention.

"Perhaps he took a cab," he muttered, adding an "excuse me" as he almost bumped into a woman as he descended the stairs into the hot and stuffy Underground station. He bought his ticket, and as soon as his feet touched the platform, a blast of air and a roar from the tunnel announced the arriving train. He boarded the last carriage and settled into his seat, glad to find himself its only passenger. The train gained speed and moved away from its stop, the white tile of the station wall soon replaced by the inky blackness of the tunnel.

As the train jostled him back and forth, Carter considered the other possibility: one of Dr. Belleville's "invisible agents from the next world" had paid him a visit.

"Bah," Carter growled out loud. He couldn't accept that... he refused to accept it. So he had two possible solutions, and neither one was logical or rational. He swore in frustration. Leaning back in his seat, he blew out a breath and gazed at his reflection in the window opposite.

A second face stared back.

Carter stifled a scream and partially rose from his seat. A quick glance around the train car showed that he was still its only passenger. The other face wasn't a reflection in the glass, but was actually hanging outside the window of the moving train, peering inside. Then Carter realized who it was—the same face he saw on that night in the desert.

The image vanished in the bright platform lights as the train slowed to a stop at Chancery Lane. Carter sprinted out of his seat and onto the platform. He decided to make the hour-long walk home in the fresh air, sunlight and safety of a bustling crowd.

His two theories about the incident at his house circled in his mind like vultures over the carcass of a dead animal as he negotiated the pedestrians on the sidewalk. He kept trying to stuff one possibility or the other into some logical form, but they refused to cooperate, squishing out of the mold. There was no luck creating a third hypothesis. So occupied was he in his thoughts that he was slightly surprised when he found himself on the stoop of his home. He had just unlocked the front door when a female voice came from behind him.

"Mr. Pinsent…"

He turned around to face May Ottley.

"Mr. Pinsent," she said, "I've been waiting in the park across the street for you to return. We need to talk."

Carter opened the door wide in invitation. His surprise at her appearance became polite coolness. "Please." She walked past him, trailing an intoxicating whiff of lavender perfume. He followed inside, closing the door behind him. "May I take your coat?"

"Thank you."

She handed the garment to Carter. After hanging it up on the hall tree, he motioned to the parlor. May went in and sat on the sofa while he took an armchair. There was silence for almost a minute.

"I read about what happened in the newspaper," she finally said. "I'm glad to see you were not harmed, although I'm sorry to hear about your father."

"Thank you. I appreciate your concern."

"Might I inquire over his condition?"

Carter's voice caught in his throat. "The doctor is not optimistic."

"I am sorry." May bit her lower lip and took a deep breath before she continued. "You see, my father is in the same hospital for the same reason."

Carter sat upright in the chair. "What? Sir Robert is the other patient?"

May nodded. "A similar incident occurred at my home."

"When?"

"The day prior to yours."

"What happened? I read nothing about it in the paper, although I confess I haven't been paying that much attention to the press the last few days," Carter said.

"There was nothing in the newspapers." May flashed a rueful smile. "Wealth has its privileges."

"I suppose."

"I attended the opera that night with my friend Lady Austin. When I returned, I found my father on the floor of the library," May said.

"Was he senseless?"

"Inanimate."

Carter leaned forward. "So you did not encounter the intruder? You didn't see it... him?"

May shook her head.

"That's good to hear." After a moment, he shook his head and sat back in his chair. "Sir Robert and my father falling into the same condition two days apart... that is unlikely to be a mere coincidence."

"And it is just as unlikely they have been struck down by same unknown disease," May said, "that for some reason has not infected us."

Carter slammed his fist against the arm of the chair in frustration. "Then what could it be? Ptahmes' curse?"

She appeared to gather up her courage. "Mr. Pinsent, we parted company in Egypt not on the best terms."

That was an understatement. Carter nodded in agreement.

"We are now in a position where working together is the best way... perhaps the only way... to obtain a solution to help both our fathers," May said.

"And we don't have much time," Carter said.

"And we don't have much time," May confirmed.

"Then I propose we forget our last... discussion outside the tomb and return to the point just prior to Dr. Belleville's arrival," Carter said. "The time when we were eating together."

"I agree... Carter." May smiled.

He returned the smile. "As do I, May."

They gazed into each other's eyes for a moment before May continued, "What happened in the temple? What did you see? It was clear you saw something."

Carter got out of the chair and nervously paced the room, debating whether or not to tell her what he had seen. He had kept up his part of the bargain by staying silent, yet the attacks made it appear that Dr. Belleville had no intention of living up to his end of agreement.

May watched in silence for a few moments before she spoke. "We have to be honest with each other, Carter. That is the only way our partnership will work."

"Yes, you're right." Carter stood behind the chair, gripping its back. "I saw Ptahmes in the tomb. The body's state of preservation was remarkable, unlike any other mummified remains I've viewed. Before I could take a closer look, Dr. Belleville and your father came into the chamber. They ordered me to keep quiet about what I had seen. Sir Robert backed the demand up with a bribe of one thousand pounds... and a gun."

May gave a slight gasp and stiffened, bringing one hand to her mouth.

Carter walked to the fireplace. He adjusted the position of a small cat figurine, one of his mother's favorites, to give himself more time to think. "Dr. Belleville was more direct. He threatened to harm... maybe kill... myself and my father if I ever spoke to anybody about Ptahmes' mummy. Not only by forces in this world, but ones from the next." He gave a snort. "Not that I believed him on that last one." He thought back to the face at the train window. Yet. He faced May. "So you can appreciate why I was not in the position to tell you anything that night."

"Yes, I understand now."

Carter returned to the chair and sat. "We were preparing to leave our dig when difficulties arose with the Department of Antiquities, something which never occurred with my parents' earlier visits. My father went to Cairo to sort things out, while I traveled to Port Said to meet him and make sure the artifacts were properly shipped. There, two thugs drugged me. When I was unconscious, they dumped me in a coffin and packed me off for a long ocean voyage. The attack here occurred the first night I had arrived home."

"Are you suggesting that my father was involved in these occurrences?" she challenged as she stood, tall and strong.

Ready to defend her father at all costs, Carter thought. He was going to have none of it, and fired back, "You name more likely suspects."

May's face softened from anger to acceptance. She nodded and sat.

"It had to have been Sir Robert or Dr. Belleville, or both. " Carter shrugged. "If those two men in Port Said were simply robbers, they would have whacked me on the head and pitched me in the harbor, not administered a sedative with a syringe. Although I can't prove it, I believe Dr. Belleville put into practice a demonstration of his influence and power... as a warning. All the parties in the little drama were probably hired by him using Sir Robert's money."

The clock in the front hall struck four, the chimes melancholy and hollow. May spoke after the last stroke finished echoing through the house.

"You know how my father had set his heart on the discovery," she murmured. "He feared that you or your father would either steal or destroy the mummy."

"Do you believe that?"

She shook her head.

"At the time, you told me that you were concerned that Sir Robert's mind was..." Carter searched for the correct word, "...slipping. That delusion would certainly be evidence of it."

"Yes, but I no longer think his was unbalanced." May took a deep breath, continuing in a hopeful tone. "He changed after leaving Egypt. My father has been so kind to me, kinder than ever before. In my life."

"And the good doctor? Is he also in London?"

She glowered. "Yes." She leaned toward Carter. "I am of the opinion he has my father under his thumb far more than I like."

"Dr. Belleville is a dangerous man," Carter stated. "Not only that, he gives me the creeps."

"As he does me, as well," May said. "But Dr. Belleville was so vital, I had to be cordial to him. I would put up with almost anything rather than cause difficulty with my father's work."

"Was vital?" Carter asked.

May stood, walked to the window and stared deeply into the gathering dusk. "We—my father, Dr. Belleville, our dragoman Hassan Ali and myself—accompanied the mummy to London. Before you ask, I don't know where the sarcophagus was taken after we landed. Dr. Belleville took up residence at our house. My father and he would disappear during the day, supposedly to study the mummy. They refused to answer any of my questions when they returned home."

"Did you actually see Ptahmes?"

"No, I still wasn't permitted to." Her voice was tinged with bitterness. She turned toward Carter. "One night, I overheard them talking in the library. Dr. Belleville was proclaiming they would have nothing to fear once they possessed a secret which granted as great a power over life and death as Providence. A mystic power, of course, connected with the discovery of Ptahmes."

Carter was incredulous. "A mystic power greater than God over life and death? That story belongs to the Middle Ages."

"Yes—but Dr. Belleville believes it. I am as sure of that as that I live."

"And is that a reason why you should give it credence, too? Dr. Belleville is perhaps a lunatic. Either that or he has made a truly wonderful discovery." Carter waved off the idea. "Which I completely doubt. That man, I fancy, is a rascal—but also a sane one. What next?"

May continued, "Two days later, however, my father and Dr. Belleville had a terrible row."

"Do you know about what?"

May shook her head. "I only heard loud, angry voices, but couldn't make out any words. Dr. Belleville moved out of the house immediately. I discovered my father on the floor the next night."

"Followed by the attack here twenty-four hours later." Carter stood and began to pace. "And there have been no further disturbances at your house?"

"No."

"What about Hassan Ali?"

"I haven't seen him since we returned from Egypt. He must be staying wherever the sarcophagus is being kept."

"The common thread running through this is Ptahmes." Carter scrubbed his fingers through his hair. "Six people know of his presence in London. Three have been attacked, two left in some type of catatonic state. I was almost strangled, and you have been spared."

"So far."

Carter took a step toward her. "Are you safe, May?"

"The butler and gardener take turns guarding my room at night."

"Good." He smiled. "Then the status of the last two people, Dr. Belleville and your dragoman, is still unknown."

"It could be that Dr. Belleville is the one holding an end of that thread," May said as she stood and moved toward Carter. "If he believes he can obtain the knowledge of some great power from Ptahmes, he may wish to remove anybody who is aware of the mummy's existence so he could retain the secret for himself."

Carter slowly circled the room. "But why the differences in the attacks? Why were our fathers put in some form of suspended animation, while I had to fight for my life?"

"You said you had just arrived at your house," May said.

"That is true."

"And your father had no idea when you were coming back?"

"None whatsoever."

"Then perhaps you were an unwelcome surprise in the plans. An upset," May suggested, "so you had to be dealt with in whatever expedient manner possible."

Carter's eyes drifted to the window as he muttered, "That could be it." Night had already descended outside. The recollection of the face from the train made him rush over to draw the curtains closed. Then it hit him—he quickly spun around and declared, "The perfume!"

"What?"

Carter went up to May. "Remember how the perfume from the sarcophagus affected me in the desert?" May nodded. "Before I was attacked here, I smelled it again. It must act on the optic nerve, or a portion of the brain, which causes hallucinations. That's why I only saw a grotesque shadow of the intruder. My mind provided his disguise.

"Dr. Belleville told me Ptahmes' body was covered with some type of oil which evaporated on contact with the air, releasing a type of gas. He also said he was planning to analyze and experiment with the substance when he returned to London. So it is possible the power he spoke of isn't 'mystical', it's chemical... some form of a drug. And he administered the first doses to our fathers."

May gasped. "You mean they are being used like some kind of laboratory animals?"

"They are unwitting participants in a wicked experiment," Carter said. "It could be that Dr. Belleville is paying hospital employees to keep track of our fathers' conditions. He told me at the temple he had 'eyes everywhere'. And that could explain why the intruder tried to kill me instead of employing the drug to put me into the same state—there wasn't any extra."

The two of them sank back into their seats, both lost in thought. The room filled with an uncomfortable stillness while they attempted to think through all they had said. Finally, May spoke.

"If it is a drug, we need to obtain a sample and take it to the hospital. The doctors could then determine if there is an antidote," she said firmly.

"That makes sense," Carter said, "but we have to get it first, and that means finding Dr. Belleville. Do you have any idea where he is now?"

"No, I don't."

"How about his own home? Any place he stays, like a club? An office for his practice?"

"No... and as far as I know, he has no current practice."

A gloomy, defeated silence fell. More minutes dragged by.

May stood. "Wait a minute! Oscar Neitenstein!"

"Who?" Carter recalled his conversation with his father in the desert when returning to his camp. "Wait, that name sounds familiar."

"He is a medium here in London and holds seances." May noted Carter's puzzled expression. "He goes into a trance..."

"Or pretends to."

"And supposedly communicates with people's relatives on the other side of the veil, giving advice about current events and even predicting the future," May went on. "Dr. Belleville took my father to a few of the gatherings. Now that I think about it, my father's interest in Ptahmes began not long after he returned from one of those sessions."

Carter sat forward in his chair and held out a cautioning hand. "Wait, wait. Are you saying that this Neitenstein chap talked to Sir Robert and Dr. Belleville about the Nile kings? Prophets and wizards and magicians and the elixir of life and Ptahmes?"

"Yes. Dr. Belleville attends those seances regularly." May looked squarely at Carter. "I shall make some inquiries. If I am correct, he will be at the next scheduled one. And so shall we."

CHAPTER NINE

*S**pook chasing must be a great way to feather one's nest*, Carter thought as he and May climbed the steps to a stately red brick building on the edge of Hyde Park. The finely carved wooden door was polished to a gleaming shine. May rang the bell, and a tall, thin butler, so pale he was almost translucent, appeared. He regarded them with watchful, colorless eyes.

"Miss Ottley and Mr. Pinsent," May crisply announced.

The butler bowed in acknowledgment and swung the door wide. Carter and May stepped into the marble-floored hallway. Removing their coats, they handed them to the silent servant. He retreated, walking as though he had a pole rammed up his backside, his legs slightly pigeon-toed and stiff like broomsticks.

Polite laughter and the tinkling of glasses drifted through the open double doors on their right. It sounded more like a party rather than a gathering of people wishing to communicate with the dead. May led the way into an opulent room decorated with silk draperies, paintings and thick woolen rugs scattered across a mirror-like wooden floor.

Six people stood in a loose circle, their champagne flutes glinting in the light of the overhead chandelier. Their expensive clothes and hand-picked jewelry marked them as members of high society. Carter felt more out of place here than he did during his first day in the boiler room on the *Star of the Mediterranean*. May, however, appeared quite at home and plunged into the group, dragging Carter along like a prize pedigree poodle.

A rapid succession of names and associations assaulted Carter as May made introductions: Lady Helen Atwater, Mrs. Greaves (wife of a Parliamentary Undersecretary) and the Count and Countess von Oeltzen (the Austrian Ambassador). A Mr. Weldon and Lord Hubbard rounded out the gathering. Carter awkwardly stood as scraps of conversations flew past him:

"Three thousand, I tell you. He cannot go on like that. Shouldn't wonder if he went abroad. Like father, like son. Old Ranger had the same passion for bridge."

"My test of a really fine soprano is the creepy feeling the high C gives one in the small of the back. Delicious. She never thrills me at all."

"My dear Mrs. Greaves, if it was not for her red hair, she would be as commonplace as—as my dear friend Mrs. Sorenson. Why men love red hair—"

"They say it will end in the divorce court. That is what comes of marrying a milkmaid. And, after all, she did not present him with a son. Ah, well, it's an ill wind that blows nobody any good. Young Carnarvon is his heir still, and his chances of succeeding grow rosier every day."

Carter almost wanted to chime in with "a funny thing happened when I was a stoker on a steamship..." but decided against it. Instead, he detached himself from the empty, pretentious twaddle and wandered away to examine an oil painting hanging on the wall. Enclosed in a heavy gilt frame, it depicted an overweight nude woman reclining on some fancy pillows, attended to by just-as-chubby flying cherubs. With a sigh, he turned around. While the high social pecking order was represented, Dr. Belleville was not.

Carter's disappointment didn't last long. Dr. Belleville strode through the doors and stopped just inside the room. He scanned the assembled guests before his gaze settled on May, giving a slight start. When he spotted Carter, his expression changed to one of discovering an unexpected, and unwelcome, surprise on the sole of his shoe. However, he made a fast recovery, and gave an affable incline of his head toward Carter, who did likewise. May then made her way towards Carter, soon joined by Dr. Belleville.

"Good evening, May," he said. "How is Sir Robert's condition?"

"Sadly, there is no change." May gestured to Carter. "Mr. Pinsent's father also suffers from the same affliction."

"Really?" Dr. Belleville glanced at Carter with cold eyes. "How very unusual."

"Isn't it?" Carter curtly replied.

"Well, Mr. Pinsent, I must say it is a surprise to see you here," Dr. Belleville said.

"Yes, I'm sure it is," Carter responded. "Fortunately, it didn't take me as long to return to London as some supposed, although the journey was arduous."

Dr. Belleville ignored the remark. "Based on what you said at the temple, I assumed you did not believe in spiritualism."

"I don't."

"Mr. Pinsent lost his mother recently," May jumped in. "I told him how highly you spoke about this medium's skills. I convinced him to set aside his disbelief in the hopes of receiving a message from her."

Dr. Belleville put on a polite smile. "Let us hope the spirits honor your request."

A gong sounded, deep and reverberating. At the same time, everybody in the room fell silent, as though admonished by the schoolmaster for talking out of turn. May turned to Carter and placed her index finger on her lips.

Another set of double doors opened by themselves, a cheap but marvelous parlor trick. The sitters funneled their way through the doorway quietly and meekly. Carter had to fight the urge to bleat like a sheep.

They entered a chamber different than the bright and cheery one they left. This room was painted entirely black. A semi-circle of a dozen red velvet upholstered chairs faced an ornate sofa, almost buried under Turkish-style throw pillows.

A carved, walnut table stood in front, blank paper and a pencil resting on top next to a single candle sitting in a gilded candle holder. Two tall candelabras, the grand type that would be in a cathedral, flanked the sofa. Only the candles illuminated the room.

Carter and May took the seats at one end of the semi-circle. Dr. Belleville sat opposite them at the far end. The rest of those attending filled in the remaining chairs as the doors closed behind them.

The gong rang a second time. A thrill ran through the room, almost like an electric current, as the people seated in the chairs excitedly exchanging glances. The show was about to commence.

Oscar Neitenstein entered the room through some black curtains. He was a tall, thin fellow, with big, black eyes, a thick-lipped mouth and a bulbous nose. His hands were beautiful, and his long, delicate fingers were covered with valuable diamond rings. Carter estimated Neitenstein's mustache and beard consisted of about at most sixteen coarse stiff black hairs: four on each side of his upper lip and eight on his chin. He plucked at the latter continually in order to display his sparkling jewelry. Neitenstein struck Carter as a man who adored himself and expected to be adored in return. A glance toward Dr. Belleville told him even that huge ego was suppressed in Neitenstein's presence. The medium took his place before the sofa.

"Ladies and gentlemen, I wish to remind you I am not a mere fortuneteller. I am a medium. I can speak to the spirits on the other side of this realm and bring you messages from the great beyond." Neitenstein spoke in a smooth baritone, but with hints of P.T. Barnum praising an elephant. "My skills were honed in the mystical lands of the Orient, where I studied under the greatest masters of the art of divination. I have traveled the world, astounding audiences with my gifts."

Carter tried to stifle a giggle and make it into a cough. He didn't completely succeed. Mrs. Greaves, the Countess and the Ambassador all in turn gave Carter scowling glances. It was as if everybody recognized and resented his skepticism. Neitenstein paid no attention to it.

"Oh, but do not be fooled by my humble demeanor, for I possess the skills of the most gifted of clairvoyants!" The medium made a sweeping gesture with his hands, the diamonds glittering in the candlelight. "My eyes view what others cannot, and my ears hear the whispers of the dead. I have communed with the departed souls of remarkable leaders and artists, from Napoleon to Shakespeare. They have taught me the secrets of the universe from their wise tongues. I bring those visions to life for you.

"Your instructions are simple. You will wait until I begin to breathe in a heavy manner, like someone in a deep sleep. Those who wish to experiment, take my hands and hold them firmly for a little while. Think of the matter next to your heart and then we shall see what we shall see."

With a smile of lordly self-confidence, he reposed his limbs upon a couch and sank back on the cushions. Carter looked around at the others and saw they stared at Neitenstein with rapt intentness.

Soon, the medium began to breathe deeply and appeared to be in a trance, his body quite limp. His audience turned and cast nervous glances at each other. They pointed at one another. Who would dare try the oracle? Everyone feared, it seemed, to be the first.

At last Count von Oeltzen arose grandly, approached and took Neitenstein's hand in his own. A breathless silence fell upon the gathering, lasting about four minutes. Neitenstein started to speak.

"I see..." The medium spoke not in his ordinary baritone, but in a high falsetto.

"That is his spirit guide," May whispered to Carter. He nodded.

"I see a short fat man in the uniform of an Austrian courier. He is seated in a railway train... smoking a cigar. He has on his knees a small, flat iron box. It contains papers... letters and dispatches. He is coming to England—"

"Ah!" sighed the Count. He stood tall in self-importance.

"He is on his way to you," Neitenstein went on. "The dispatches are for you. One of them is in a cipher. It relates to your recall. It—"

The Count dropped Neitenstein's hands as if they burnt him and backed away, his face a mask of shock. The apparently soon-to-be ex-diplomat composed himself and offered his wife his arm. She rose gracefully from the chair and looped her arm through his; without a word they marched out of the room with dignified strides.

For a little while everybody sat under a sort of spell. At last, Mrs. Greaves arose and moved to the couch. Presently the high falsetto squeaked forth again.

"I see—a large building, square, very tall. It is made of steel and stone. It is in America—in New York. It is a hotel. In it, a room. There are tables and chairs. One—two—three—four—five—six are there. They play cards. The game is poker. One loses. He is young. He is English. He has a little cast in his right eye. His name is Julian Greaves. The floor is littered with cards. Julian Greaves is annoyed because he loses." The voice ceased.

Mrs. Greaves released the medium's hands and turned to the people seated. She was smiling—a forced, brave smile. "I believe that my naughty son is at present occupied exactly as you have heard described. Good night, I—" She left before she finished speaking.

The remaining participants threw glances at each other. Carter and Dr. Belleville locked eyes, almost in a dare. Dr. Belleville stirred as though to rise. Carter immediately got to his feet.

"It is my turn, I suppose." Carter attempted to inject some humor. "I will step forward and risk the darkest secret of my life being laid bare to one and all here assembled." Carter took the few steps to reach the sofa, then held the medium's hands. "Who knows, perhaps I'll find out where my watch is."

Neitenstein answered the question instantly, and in his natural voice. "It was sold on the streets of Port Said to a worker for the Egyptian government."

Startled, Carter wondered if it was just possible that this fellow had some esoteric faculty after all. Science, of course, scouted around the edges of the phenomena of clairvoyance, but Carter wasn't quite the believer in it as the others in the room. But he was beginning to become one.

Carter looked over his shoulder to May, trying to keep his tone light. "And I think I know who that was... a gentleman from the Office of Antiquities."

He turned back to the medium and was shocked by what he saw. Neitenstein's chest heaved with a desperate gasp for air and his face twisted into a deathly fish-like pallor, white-yellow in color. His eyelids peeled open, revealing two marble eyes locked on some unseen terror above him. He was an image of pure monstrosity.

The participants shifted to the edge of their seats, leaning forward, barely breathing as they waited for the manifestations to commence. After what seemed like an eternity had passed, Neitenstein moved uneasily then groaned in pain as a spasm spread through his body, clamping down on Carter's hands with such force that Carter winced. The air around him was almost tangible with tension.

The medium's mouth moved. It contorted in a desperate struggle as if the lips and tongue were controlled by someone or something out of practice with their use. Inarticulate sounds spilled from Neitenstein, slowly forming into what could be garbled syllables of a language that was vaguely familiar, although Carter couldn't quite place it. The words resembled Arabic, but not the version he spoke. Perhaps it was an archaic dialect—long forgotten and buried in time.

The speech stopped, and Neitenstein fell silent. With a sudden spasmodic writhe and twist, he broke away from Carter and sat erect. He shook like a man with a violent fever, and he began to pant and groan like a wounded animal. His hands groped in front of him.

"By Jove, he looks like he wants to write something!" Mr. Weldon said.

Carter placed the pencil in Neitenstein's hand and guided it to the blank paper. He stepped back from the table. The medium started to write. Each movement of the pencil brought forth an array of scribbles, cascading down the page with such fervor that Carter wondered if the pen would rip through the sheet. But no words appeared, only symbols.

"Hieratic script," Carter murmured to himself, casting a look at Dr. Belleville from the corner of his eye. The doctor was practically standing now, transfixed by the hieroglyphs being transcribed onto the page.

Neitenstein erupted in a loud groan, and he hurled the pencil across the room. He began to thrash violently on the sofa, but Carter quickly stepped in and grasped Neitenstein's arms. Neitenstein's body went limp as if all of the energy had drained from him at once. Carter eased the medium back down on the couch into the ocean of pillows.

A savage gust of wind—violent, hot—blew into the room. Gritty, invisible, stinging grains of sand filled the air, reminding Carter of the vicious Khamsih winds he had experienced in Egypt. Both candelabras swayed and then tumbled to the ground with a clanging crash, candles going out and rolling over the floor. The candle on the table shot away and its flickering flame was snuffed out. The phantom sandstorm howled and clawed its way through the room as darkness engulfed it like a heavy blanket.

Pandemonium flared. Lady Helen's piercing scream rent the air as if cut by a hot knife. All around the blacked-out room, voices blended together into a chorus demanding light and answers at the same time.

A beating of wings, as though from a large bird, circled Carter's head. The wind lifted the loose piece of paper on the table and flung it straight into his face. Startled, he grabbed it and stumbled backwards until he encountered May's knees, then he thrust the paper behind him and rattled it. "May!" he commanded through gritted teeth.

Her hand pressed against his back as she took it from him. He moved back to the sofa. Then, just as suddenly as it had begun, the storm dissipated, leaving a chilling quiet in its wake. The unearthly silence was broken by a shout.

"Look!" a man yelled. It sounded like Lord Hubbard.

A pale, white face, almost luminous, floated in the dark. It hovered about six feet above the ground, staring out with a blank expression. Its features were immobile, like those of a doll or mannequin. Lady Helen's scream filled the air once again.

There were some metallic clicks, like pulling the trigger of an empty revolver. A few sparks glittered in the darkness. A candle flared up, grasped in the hand of the butler. He had a pistol in the other. Carter tensed, then realized the weapon was actually one of the new Pist-O-Liter lighters.

The servant righted one candelabra, lighting the two candles remaining in their holders with the one he held. One candle was cracked and tilted at an angle, while the other flickered weakly. Surveying the participants with an icy stare, he left without a word, his slippered feet soundless against the polished floor.

Neitenstein was sprawled out on the pillows, deep in slumber. The steady rise and fall of his chest suggested he was comfortably relaxed. May moved closer to Carter and faced at Dr. Belleville.

"You may wish to check Mr. Neitenstein, doctor, given what just occurred," she said.

Dr. Belleville grunted a response and shuffled to the sofa. Bending down, he carefully inspected the unconscious medium. When he finally straightened up, the others stepped nearer in expectation. "In my professional opinion," he said, his voice self-important with authority, "he is in a hypnotic sleep and not in any danger. He will awaken naturally." His eyes swept across the table, and he pointed. "Where is the paper that was there?"

Carter shrugged. "The wind must have blown it away."

Dr. Belleville's glared at Carter. His face a study in frustration, he stalked around the room, searching under the chairs and kicking aside the scattered candles. When his search yielded no results, he spun on his heel and strode back to Carter.

"What is so important about the paper, Doctor?" Lady Helen asked.

"Because it contained—" he started to shout, but he stopped himself. After a deep breath, he smiled before speaking again in a controlled way. "Because I think it included a significant communication to me from the other side. I believe it contained very vital, personal information…"—he shifted his gaze to Carter and spoke in a guttural tone, controlling his fury with great effort—"for *me*. You were standing right by the table when the candles were extinguished, young man. You must have it."

"I'm afraid you are mistaken." Carter held his arms out from his sides. "You may search me if you wish. Go ahead, turn out all my pockets. I give my permission."

"You may search me, too, Dr. Belleville," May said.

"Oh, yes, do search me as well," Lady Helen giggled.

May's sweeping gesture took in the room. "As well as everybody else. Any one of us had the opportunity to take the paper while the room was in darkness."

"Of course, it may not be in any of our pockets, because I could have eaten it." Carter winked at Lady Helen. "Like all spies do."

The room filled with mocking titters. His eyes ablaze, Dr. Belleville shot Carter a venomous glare. He clenched his fists, then forced a smile on his face and quipped, "I do hope he used salt on it!" The others roared with laughter, including Dr. Belleville himself, laughing a little too hard.

"Well, this has been quite the evening," Lady Helen said after she resumed her composure. "I don't know when I've been so enthralled!"

"Without a doubt! Quite true, quite true," declared the other sitters, and their voices filled the room. The night's entertainment over, the guests drifted out of the room. They chatted among themselves as though they had just viewed a play at the Theatre

Royal. Carter, May, Dr. Belleville and the sleeping Neitenstein were all who remained when the doors shut behind the others. The doctor glared at Carter and May.

"I do hope you get your message, doctor," Carter said politely. "Perhaps the spirits should try a wire the next time. I find it so much more reliable."

Dr. Belleville looked as if he was about to explode.

"Good evening, Dr. Belleville." May took Carter's arm and escorted him to the entry hall. The butler was already waiting by the front door, holding their coats. He helped May with hers. "Thank you."

Carter took his coat and spoke to the butler. "You may wish to attend to Mr. Neitenstein."

The butler nodded as he opened the door. Carter and May stepped outside and went down the steps to the street.

"Keep walking and don't say anything," Carter said out of the corner of his mouth. "We may be watched."

"Hail a cab," May responded in an equally quiet voice. "We'll go to my townhome."

"There's one!" Carter held out his arm and yelled. "Cabbie!"

A black cab pulled up. They climbed into the back seat, and May gave the driver an address in Kensington. The cab pulled away from the curb. She pulled out the crumpled sheet of paper from her purse, spreading it open on her lap. She tapped the page with one finger.

"It seems we have a translation task in front of us," May said.

CHAPTER TEN

The taxi halted in front of a beautiful, white four-story stone house, separated from the bustle of the street by a wrought-iron fence. Two bay windows flanked the entry door, their elliptical tops arcing out. They were matched by another pair marking the second floor. Smaller windows lined the third level and three dormer windows poked through the front of the Mansard roof.

Carter and May went up the steps, the ornate entry door opening as they reached the stoop, held by a middle-aged, balding, stout man.

"Good evening, miss," the butler said as the two entered.

"Good evening, Matthews," May replied as she removed her coat. "Any word from the hospital?"

"I'm afraid not, miss."

An expression of sadness flashed on her face. "Mr. Pinsent and I will be working in the library. Bring us some coffee, please."

"Very well, miss." Matthews took their coats. He noiselessly retreated across the hallway's black-and-white checkerboard marble floor, disappearing through an archway at the far end.

A staircase, with iron railings and a beige carpet, ran up one side of the hall, creating the impression of ascending to a throne room. Oil and watercolor paintings of ancient Egyptian scenes in bright reds, oranges, blues and golds adorned the light blue walls. May led Carter to a door at the base of the stairs. She opened it and let him through.

They entered the library, a room stretching from the front to the back of the house. The bay windows faced the street while two other enormous ones filled the rear wall. Mahogany bookcases reaching the ceiling lined the remaining walls, interrupted only by a fireplace containing a crackling fire. A rectangular table took up most of the space in the middle of the floor.

May placed the crumpled paper on the table and smoothed it out. She stared at it for a moment. Carter joined her.

"It's a mess." Carter shifted the sheet's position to get a better look at it. "The hieroglyphs are not completely formed, others are sloppy, with some I don't even recognize. They might be random marks of the pencil, for that matter."

May nodded in agreement. "This resembles a message scribbled in a rush because the writer believed he didn't have much time."

"The writer knew?" Carter looked at her with one eyebrow arched. "So you think this was a note dashed off from a spook on the other side of the veil? From the realm of the dead?"

May met his gaze evenly. "Don't you? You have to acknowledge it is a possibility. After all, you witnessed what occurred at the seance. Oscar Neitenstein even provided you information about your watch that he couldn't have known previously."

"Well, that's true enough," Carter admitted. "My opinion always has been that conversing with the great beyond, or clairvoyance, or whatever you want to call it, was a sham at worst and coincidence at best. But after tonight…" He shrugged off the rest of the sentence and shook his head. "This is a short… communication, I guess I'll call it… but the condition is poor. It will take some time and effort to translate. How do we start?"

May opened a drawer in the table and removed blank sheets of paper, pencils and pens. "Champollion's *Dictionnaire égyptien en écriture hiéroglyphique*, *Précis du système hiéroglyphique des anciens Égyptiens*, and *Grammaire égyptienne* are on the bottom shelf of the bookcase to the left of the window," she directed.

Carter went to fetch them. "I assume you have Brugsch's *Hieroglyphisch-demotisches Wörterbuch*?"

May nodded as she began to remove the texts from another set of shelves and place them on the tabletop. "All seven volumes."

Carter stacked his books next to hers as well. "Sharpe's *Egyptian hieroglyphics*?"

"Behind you, third shelf from the top." May pulled two chairs up to the table and sat in one. Carter took the second chair. She glanced at him and smiled. "Move closer. You can't see well from there. Don't worry. Contrary to impression I might give sometimes, I don't bite."

Carter returned the smile and scooted his seat nearer. The door opened, and Matthews entered. He placed the silver coffee service next to the books.

"Do you require anything else before I retire, miss?" the butler asked.

"Mr. Pinsent will be spending the night. Please prepare the Green Room for his use," May said.

"Certainly, miss."

"Thank you, Matthews. That is all. Good night."

Matthews bowed slightly. "Baxter will remain outside your door tonight, miss. Good night. Good night, sir." He padded out of the room, softly closing the door.

May noted Carter's surprised expression and smiled. "You yourself said this process may take some time. The Green Room is quite comfortable."

The two began to work. They sat at the large table, discussing and debating meanings for the various symbols. Open books spilled over onto the floor, papers containing drawings of possible variations of the ones found in the message littered the surface, and steaming coffee cups formed a crooked line along the edge. Even after a few hours, only about half of the hieroglyphs had revealed their definitions.

Carter put down his pen and pushed himself away from their work with a tired groan. "My eyes are starting to cross. I have to take a break." He stood and stretched, then nodded toward their work. "You are excellent with the structure and grammar."

"Thank you. And you demonstrate a remarkable sight vocabulary of hieroglyphs. You don't need to consult the dictionaries much." May went to the pot, draining the last drop of coffee.

"I thank you. My mother had a facility for languages—she was fluent in four and spoke three others to a lesser degree. I always enjoyed the reactions when we were in Egypt and this red-haired, blue-eyed Irish woman spoke flawless Arabic." Carter laughed at the memory. "She taught me and introduced hieroglyphs to me when I was a child. It was like a game. We'd write notes to each other with them. I hope I've inherited some of that gift of language from her. I suppose you learned from Sir Robert."

May took her coffee cup to the window and gazed out into the night. "My father possesses no knowledge of hieroglyphs."

"But Sir Robert's fame as a scholar and an Egyptologist... for translating papyri..." Carter's voice trailed off at the implications of what he was saying set in. "Wait... are you telling me... it was you? You did all the real work?"

May's lack of a response shouted the answer.

"He... you... do you mean to tell me..." Carter sputtered in anger. "In other words, without you, Sir Robert would be unknown! A nothing!"

"That is not true," May responded. "He is quite knowledgeable about ancient Egypt."

"But he reaped all the credit from your translations! You are three times the scholar he is!" He paced the floor, raking his fingers through his hair, not upset with May, but with Sir Robert. "He's used you as... as a servant and secretary because he could get no other to serve him as well and intelligently!"

"Carter, please understand. I permitted it. I offered it freely."

"Why, May? Why allow it?" Carter went up to her. "There are women Egyptologists... like Margaret Benson, Mary Brodrick and Nora Griffith."

There was a long silence before she answered in a soft voice. "Your mother recently passed away, but she was an important part of your life for many years. As for me, my mother walked out on my father when I was a baby. I was raised by a succession of nannies. I never saw my mother, never knew her. To my knowledge, she's never contacted me, or even attempted to. I have no idea where she lives... it could be in the south of France, for all I know."

"I see," Carter said.

"Do you?" May asked with a wry smile.

"I believe so," Carter said. He worked up his courage to ask the next question. "Forgive me—is your father very much attached to you?"

May gave a slight shake of her head. "No—his heart and soul are wrapped up in his work. I devoted myself to learning hieroglyphs when I was ten... as a way obtain admittance into his world and his acceptance. To gain his affection."

"And yet you still love him."

"More than all the world. My father is all I have," she answered.

"We're the same in many ways," Carter observed quietly. "We both have fathers, but in some ways, we are still orphans."

After a sad nod, May glanced at the clock on the mantle. She said brightly, trying to clear the gloom from the conversation, "My! It's 2 am already. Perhaps we should start again in the morning."

"Yes, that's a good idea," Carter said, grateful for an escape from the awkward conversation.

"Allow me to show you to your room." May headed toward the door.

"What about all this?" Carter waved one hand over their work on the table. "I'm certain Dr. Belleville knows one of us has the paper from the seance. I am just as certain if I went home now, I'd find signs of a burglar's visit."

"What does it matter? He cannot read hieroglyphs."

"That may be true, but he could hire some student at the university, or just destroy the document to prevent us from translating it," Carter noted.

"That is very clear thinking, Carter. Let us cover our tracks then." May gathered up the papers. "Please shelve the books."

Carter began returning the volumes of books to their appropriate spots. May moved away from the table and stepped up to the fireplace, reaching for the painting above the mantle. With a gentle tug, it swung open on its concealed hinges, revealing a shiny metal wall safe. May entered the combination, placed their work inside then shut the heavy door and returned the art to its original place. By the time Carter finished, May had swept the pens and pencils into the drawer.

"There." She smiled with satisfaction. "Nobody will know what we did tonight."

Carter grinned in response, then followed May as she led the way upstairs. On the second floor, she pointed to a door.

"That is your room. Mine is at the front of the house. I'll see you in the morning. Breakfast is at eight. Good night, Carter," she smiled.

"Good night, May."

For a moment, they both lingered as if they didn't want to part. At last, May walked down the hall and Carter stepped into the bedroom.

The Green Room lived up to its name. The walls were painted a rich and vibrant jade. The four-poster canopy bed was dressed in an emerald satin spread, piled high with pillows. Heavy drapes, woven of thick green silk and edged with tassels, hung by a set of French doors that opened onto the balcony overlooking the rear gardens. A cheery fire burned in the small fireplace.

Carter closed the door and strode over to the bed, a smile playing on his lips as he saw the pristine pair of silk nightclothes that had been laid out for him. He shunted them aside, now preferring the comfort of sleeping in just his undershorts—the same way he had slept for so many nights on the freighter. He discarded his clothes on a nearby chair, topped by the pajamas. Most of the pillows ended on the floor and he plumped up the remaining one.

He switched off the light, the bedroom suddenly awash in soft, blue-gray light from the full moon streaming through the closed French doors. He considered closing the drapes but decided against it and climbed into the plush bed. As he settled, he released a long, satisfied sigh. His eyes shut as sleep pulled him under.

Something jolted from his slumber. He turned his head and squinted at the bedside clock, barely able to make out the time in the moonlight: 3:45 am. The same sensation he had on the Nile steamer ran through him: somebody was in the room.

He glanced around the dim chamber. The room was still and empty. That feeling must have been a dream. He shook his head and let out a short laugh. "You're being silly," he said to himself. He closed his eyes and was about to drift off when something stirred beneath the comforter. It moved again. With a start, he realized what it was.

The slithering scales of a snake crawled up his left leg.

CHAPTER ELEVEN

Carter's heart raced like a runaway locomotive, pounding against his rib cage with such force he thought it would burst through at any moment. He wanted to believe this was a nightmare, or an ill-fated prank of some kind, but no matter how hard he tried he could not convince himself either way. If it was indeed a serpent, he had no idea if it was venomous or not, although he thought it most unlikely a harmless garter snake could have wandered into his bed. Best not to take any chances. That left him with only one thing he could do: nothing. One wrong twitch could trigger an attack.

He controlled his breath, hoping that not even the slightest gasp would startle the reptile. He tensed and quivered with the effort of remaining motionless as the snake moved up his body.

Carter clamped his mouth shut, his breathing shallow, perspiration moistening his forehead. The snake's strong muscles contracted and stretched as it crept up onto his abdomen. After a short pause, it began its trek toward his neck, its rough skin rasping along his bare chest.

He fought the urge to scream, throw the covers off and leap out of bed. Doing that, he knew, could sign his death warrant. He had to lie absolutely still. His eyes fixed on the narrow bulge under the quilt as it slithered nearer and nearer. Carter's fingers dug into the mattress.

The snake's head emerged from beneath the bedclothes, and it reared up, swaying hypnotically from side to side, its tongue darting in and out of its mouth. It flattened its neck, and its two hoods spread wide.

It was a cobra.

The snake paused as its cold eyes stared into Carter's face, and for a long moment, they were locked in a battle of wills—him hoping not to be bitten, the reptile deciding whether to strike. The cobra opened its mouth, baring its fangs. It hissed.

Carter wondered if he could roll, fling the covers over the cobra's head and get off the bed before the snake could strike. He started to inch his right hand to one side.

The cobra closed its mouth, dropped down and moved up Carter's neck, wrapping around his chin and sliding along his face. Its rough scales cut against his skin as it continued, almost caressing him with its forked tongue flicking in and out. The snake changed directions, moving to the edge of the bed. Dangling over the side, it slid to the floor with a soft plop.

Carter carefully rolled on his side and looked down. The cobra was coiled on the rug. He slid out of bed on the far side and crept to the fireplace, hugging the wall. Grasping the cold iron handle of the shovel from the andiron set on the hearth, he retraced his steps.

He lay prone on the mattress, his eyes locked on the serpent. The serpent began to stir. Carter raised the shovel above his head with both hands, blade pointing downwards. The snake slithered closer and closer to the bed. Carter brought the tool down like a guillotine, severing the cobra's head in one clean strike.

Carter dropped the shovel on the wooden floor, rolled onto his back and exhaled heavily. Feeling a chilly draft, he sat up and spotted that the French doors stood ajar. They were shut when he climbed into bed. He got to his feet and went to examine them. The night air was brisk as he stepped outside and peered over the balustrade. There, spread out on the lawn below, was an extended ladder and empty burlap bag next to it.

Since cobras don't climb ladders, someone must have taken it from the garden shed to access his room, and then left him a nasty surprise. He retreated into the room and pushed the French doors closed before locking them, double-checking that they were secure.

Carter viewed the remains for the snake. "Thoughtful guests always tidy up after themselves," he said to himself. Dumping the head and body of his unwanted bedmate into the small trash basket, he returned the shovel to its place then crawled into bed.

The enticing aroma of freshly cooked bacon led Carter to the sunny breakfast room the next morning. May was already seated.

"Good morning." She smiled and waved a hand at the serving dishes on the sideboard. "Please help yourself."

"Good morning and thank you." Carter picked up an empty plate and heaped it with scrambled eggs, bacon, toast and baked beans. He took the full dish to the table and sat.

"Did you sleep well?" May lifted the coffee pot and poured a cup for Carter.

"Not that well." Carter salted his eggs. "I had a visitor."

May put the coffee pot down. "A visitor?"

"Yes—" A woman's scream from upstairs interrupted Carter. "I believe your upstairs maid just found it."

"It?"

"Somebody entered my room last night through the French doors," Carter said, "and slipped a cobra under the covers."

May's cup clattered as she replaced it on the saucer. "A cobra! Do you think it was Dr. Belleville's doing?"

Carter nodded as he chewed some bacon.

May stood, placing her napkin on the table in a business-like way. "I doubt he has knowledge about the safe, and certainly not the combination, but I'll check the library anyway. Please continue with your breakfast." May left and returned in a few minutes, then took her seat. Spreading her napkin on her lap, she resumed eating. "Nothing has been disturbed."

"Which indicates Dr. Belleville had us followed here last night, understands we have the paper and wants to slow us down. But instead of destroying the document, he decided to destroy me." Carter tried to sound nonchalant, but his hand trembled as he buttered some toast.

May looked at him, concerned. She tried to match Carter's attempt at a light tone. She, too, failed. "By all means, we mustn't let that situation occur."

"I most wholeheartedly agree."

The two continued their meals in silence, the only noise their forks clinking against the china. Neither one of them looked at the other, the threat posed by Dr. Belleville filling the space between them. When they finished eating, each took a cup of coffee to the library. Without saying anything, Carter pulled the necessary books from the shelves while May retrieved the papers from the safe. They took their places at the table and plunged back into work.

A few hours later, Carter leaned back in his chair. He tossed his pencil on the table and examined the result of their labors strewn in front of them. "I don't think we can go any further," he groaned, rubbing his eyes. "We've translated some words, but the other marks just seem like scribbles... nothing resembling referenced hieroglyphs. Just our luck the messenger from the dead had particularly bad penmanship."

May nodded. "There aren't any grammatically complete sentences, either. At least, none that I can discern. Just phrases and words."

Carter dropped his hands and drummed his fingers on the table. "Well, you suggested that whatever entity wrote this didn't have much time. That would account for the message being truncated, like when sending a wire. One that got garbled in transmission, at that."

She thought for a moment. "How about this? Let's copy each word on a separate piece of paper. Then we can arrange them, rearrange them and so forth, to see if that reveals some meaning."

"Good idea." Carter scooped up the books and shelved them. May jotted down the words in a pocket-sized journal, then flicked out sheets of paper and lined them up across the tabletop like cards dealt in a game. They repeatedly swapped the slips of paper, moving them here and there, trying to order them into something meaningful. Half an hour passed.

"I think that's got it." May read the results. "'It is not meet that... wicked unbeliever... wake me from my sleep... Ka not be permitted... get papyrus.'"

Neither said anything as they considered the message. Carter paced the library, mumbling the words to himself. He stopped and spun around toward May. "Wait a minute!"

He ran back to the table and read the words again. He was so excited he had to take a deep breath to calm himself down. "I do believe this is a message to us from the world of the dead... *from* Ptahmes. And he's asking for our help."

CHAPTER TWELVE

"From Ptahmes?" May asked.

"Hear me out." Carter took a few steps as he gathered his thoughts. "Christianity holds the belief of a single soul... one per customer. But the ancient Egyptians' system was more complex."

May nodded. "They believed a person's essence, or soul, was not a lone entity, but was made up of several parts, each with its own purpose and destiny."

"Right. There was the Ka, an individual's life force or vital essence, if you prefer." Carter started walking around the room. "It was considered to be a spiritual double of the person and was closely tied to the physical body. The Ka continued to live on after death. Also, we both have witnessed a shadowy figure..."

"That could be the Sheut, another part of the soul," May said.

Carter nodded. "Then there was the Ba... it was associated with a person's personality and individuality."

"Correct. The Ba could travel between the realms of the living and the dead," May said. "It often appeared as a bird with a human head in tomb paintings."

Carter stopped and looked at May. "While we were at the seance, I could have sworn I felt the brushing of wings around my head... during the time when everything was dark and that wind was blowing through the room. Maybe it was the Ba."

May sat up in her chair. "Are you suggesting that Ptahmes' Ba was trying to communicate with you?"

Carter took his seat again. "I'm not only suggesting it, I'm getting bloody close to saying it."

May gave a half-smile. "Why, Mr. Pinsent, it does sound like you are quite starting to believe in the spirit world."

"Perhaps not completely, but I'm not rejecting it out of hand anymore, either. I think we can assume Neitenstein doesn't understand any hieroglyphs, but it doesn't really matter if he does or not. For example, I could deliver a written message to you in French, even if I didn't speak the language." He leaned back in the chair. "But we do need to rule out fraud. It's possible Neitenstein could have memorized the hieroglyphs for our benefit, in order to put on a grand show. Was he aware we were attending the seance that night?"

"I doubt it. People have to be 'in the know', if you understand, when he holds seances," May replied. "He doesn't run adverts in the papers and take reservations."

"I'm not a medical man, but I'd swear he wasn't playacting that... seizure he experienced before he began writing. If it was, he's missed his calling. He should be on the stage. Well, if there were no magic tricks involved..." Carter threw up his hands. "As much as I hate to admit this, as much as it defies my logical thought, as daft as I think it is, I'm going to have to accept Ptahmes' Ba used Neitenstein to deliver that message to us. As a medium, Neitenstein was a conduit for communication from the great beyond. He was nothing more than the postman." He leaned forward. "Look at the words again."

May stared at the papers distributed on the table. "'It is not meet that... wicked unbeliever... wake... from... sleep... not be p ermitted... get papyrus,'" May read again. She moved the two slips apart and thought for a minute. "'It is not meet that' blank,"—she tapped the space separating the two—"'wicked unbeliever'. An article must go here, like 'the' or 'a'. 'It is not meet that *a* wicked unbeliever'..." She looked up at Carter. "Dr. Belleville?"

"Sounds like a good bet."

May took out a fresh sheet of paper and pen. She started to write. "'It is not meet that a wicked unbeliever... wake... from... sleep.'" She paused for a second. "A verb construction is likely for the first space, along the lines of 'be allowed to' or 'should'. The following two blanks have to be pronouns, such as 'me' and 'my', if this is indeed a communication from Ptahmes. Let's go with the possessive." She jotted down the words. "The next one... another noun or pronoun, plus an auxiliary verb, then the last one..." She sat back in her chair. "The most obvious would be the infinitive version of 'get' or 'obtain'." She finished making notes on the page.

"What does it say now?" Carter asked.

May picked up the paper and read: "'It is not meet that a wicked unbeliever should wake me from my sleep. He cannot be permitted to get the papyrus.'" She handed the paper to Carter. He glanced over it. "You're correct. This message is from Ptahmes. Even if we change the pronouns, it's certainly about Ptahmes."

"Perhaps the intended receiver of the communique was Dr. Belleville, as he believed." Carter shook his head and replaced the page on the table. "That strikes me as strange given the content."

May thought for a second. "So if Ptahmes' Ba is still active in the spirit world, it must mean the other aspects of his soul—for instance, the Ka and the Sheut—are also, and have not been reunited with his physical body. Therefore, we can assume that Ptahmes has not been reanimated."

"Then his mummy is as dead as any other ones on display at the British Museum." Carter rubbed his chin with his index finger.

"And, we can infer from this message that he doesn't wish to be revived by somebody like Dr. Belleville." May leaned back in her chair. "What does 'he should not be permitted to get the papyrus' mean?"

"Just that." Carter stood, walked to the fireplace and stared into the flames for a moment before speaking. "It may be... and I'm just thinking out loud here... Dr. Belleville and Sir Robert drew some incorrect conclusions. Although Ptahmes had been underground for around 4000 years, Neitenstein led them to expect to find the prophet still alive and kicking. Or at least, in a slumber from which he'd awake after a few nudges in the ribs. But they were mistaken. Ptahmes was a corpse, and additional assistance is required to return him to the land of the living. I mean, even Jesus didn't resurrect himself. He had outside help."

"So there must be another papyrus which holds the key to actually revive Ptahmes," May said. "Perhaps it contains a ritual, such as are found in the *Book of the Dead*."

"Or some type of drug formulation." Carter leaned against the mantle. "According to Dr. Belleville, Ptahmes was coated with a special oil that preserved the body. The oil is quite volatile when exposed to air. In its gaseous state, it triggers hallucinations, and who knows what else. Dr. Belleville may have been successful in analyzing and experimenting with it, distilling it into a liquid, like a serum. In that form, it may induce a form of suspended animation."

"Which he injected into our fathers," May added grimly.

Carter moved away from the mantle. "It makes sense. Being a medical man, Dr. Belleville most likely experimented with the drug on animals first and observed the results. Then he needed to move onto human subjects and the argument he had with Sir Robert provided the first one. Not only that, it removed a potential enemy at the same time."

"And I was not injected because I attended the opera that night." May dropped her eyes to the table. "I shouldn't have left him alone. Maybe if I were..."

"Stop talking like that," Carter said gently. He placed his hand on hers. "Your presence or absence had nothing to do with it. If you had been home, you would have experienced the same fate."

May gazed at him, her lips curving into a gentle smile that radiated gratitude. Her beauty struck Carter like a masterfully painted portrait, every line and feature perfectly crafted to create a stunning image. It was as though he was beholding a work of art come to life, captivating and breathtaking in its perfection. He grew awkward, not really knowing what to do next. He cleared his throat and stood.

Walking to the library's rear windows, his gaze swept over the beautiful, manicured garden. Its peace and beauty seemed so out of place compared to what the two were discussing. "Next up was my father," he said. "Subject number two and also a possible obstacle. Dr. Belleville didn't expect me to be back in London—his surprise when saw me at the seance proved that—so he hadn't prepared for my presence at home and tried to get me out of the way by killing me, as you suggested."

"Why hasn't he attempted to finish what he has started?" May asked. "Put you and I into suspended animation, as the next subjects?"

Carter walked the length of the room as he thought over the question. "Perhaps he was worried four afflicted people would be too many. Two cases with similar symptoms might be considered a coincidence. Unusual, to be sure, but a coincidence nonetheless. Four could indicate a potentially contagious disease, especially since all of us were in the same region of Egypt at the same time. That would increase questions about the expeditions and trigger a closer investigation, possibly interfering with Dr. Belleville's plans. And if the tabloids got wind of it, it could set off a panic about an unknown sickness…"—he gave a rueful chuckle—" …or stories about an ancient Egyptian curse. The doctor wouldn't want any more undue attention from either situation."

"So if Dr. Belleville developed a serum from the oil which puts people into a catatonic state, then it is logical he would require a drug to reverse the process, also needed to revive Ptahmes. The formula must be written on another papyrus. That's why Ptahmes wants us to gain possession of it. He doesn't want Dr. Belleville to use it on him," May said.

"But where is it? It's like searching for a purple grain of sand in the desert." Carter sat with a sigh as the enormity of the problem dropped on him. He shrugged. "The papyrus may not even exist any longer, for all we know."

"Don't be discouraged. I believe it still exists."

"Fine, but where to start? It could be anywhere on earth."

May shook her head. "I don't think so. It must be here in London, or nearby."

He glanced at her. "What makes you say that?"

"We agree Ptahmes' soul—or souls—reside in the spirit world, a realm which has most likely operates under different rules of time and space than ours. If indeed they have any temporal or spatial constraints at all. From Ptahmes' viewpoint, he may know the precise location of the papyrus." May tapped on the paper. "That wasn't a random communication. Ptahmes directed the communication specifically to us. Here. Now. There must be a rationale."

"So it would make no sense for him to do that if the writings have been destroyed, or are located in some other part of the world," Carter said. "But why did he leave out important details? Like where to search? At least he could have been more helpful and passed on a clue."

"We both think it was a rushed message, so perhaps Ptahmes exhausted his time or energy, like running out of money at a telephone box." May sat up straight in her chair. She took a piece of paper, scribbled a few words and slid it toward Carter. "Here's something."

Carter cast a puzzled glance at May and picked up the note. It read: "Somebody outside rear window." He nodded and dropped it on the table. "That's very interesting. I'll do something about it. Tell me more."

May began to ramble, stalling, until Carter reached the window. His expression hardened as he grabbed the windowsill and pulled it open in one quick motion. A lanky boy of about fifteen years, dressed in shabby clothes, crouched down beneath the frame. Carter shot out one hand and took a firm grasp on his tattered collar.

"'Ere, lay off!" The youth flinched as Carter hung on tightly. "I ain't doin' nuffin'!"

"You should come inside," Carter retorted, "so much easier to listen."

The teen wrenched free and sprinted across the garden toward the rear wall. Carter hurled himself out of the window and took off after him. His hand caught on the intruder's shoulder, spinning him with such force they both tumbled onto the lawn. The two wrestled ferociously, fists flying, kicking up dust and debris as they rolled among the flower beds, crushing the delicate blooms.

The teen's hand closed around a nearby rock, lifting it high into the air. With one swift motion, he slammed it against Carter's head. Sparks filled his vision as he grunted and released his hold. The other boy got to his feet and continued toward the back of the property.

Carter stood, swaying a little from the blow. The intruder was halfway up the rear wall, and with a burst of speed, Carter lunged after him. As soon as he disappeared on the far side, Carter followed, scrambling up and over.

He dropped to the cobblestones of a lane running behind the houses. His prey was already rounding the far corner and disappearing from sight.

Charging after him, Carter reached the busy cross street. He glanced up and down the block, catching his breath, and spotted the youth walking rapidly down the sidewalk.

"Hey! You there! Stop!" Carter shouted.

The intruder spun around, saw Carter then tore through the crowd. Carter ran after him, jumping and sliding through the pedestrians like a lion in pursuit of a gazelle.

With a fierce determination, the other teen swerved sharply and darted into the chaotic traffic. Without hesitation, Carter propelled himself off the pavement, plunging into the raging river of trams, horse-drawn wagons and taxis. Desperate to catch up, he dodged and weaved through the vehicles, barely avoiding collisions as angry shouts and curses filled the air. When he reached the opposite sidewalk, Carter frantically scanned the sea of bodies for his target, but it was too late—the elusive intruder had seamlessly blended into the bustling city crowds.

Carter swore as he brushed off his clothes. With one final glance around, he returned to May's house. She waited for him at the top of the stoop.

"He got away," Carter answered her unspoken question as he entered the front hall and turned toward the library.

"Are you all right?" May asked.

Carter nodded as he collapsed into a chair. "I think we can assume Dr. Belleville will know everything we were talking about in a very short time."

"So we must begin the search for the papyrus at once." May took another seat.

"Phew. How long is a piece of string? Where do we start?" Carter grumbled. After a second, he asked, "At the risk of being obvious, you don't have any additional papyri here?"

"No. When a translation is completed, it is stored at the Egyptian Club," May said. "The stele is still here, but it only offered clues to the tomb's location. Not specific on any procedures."

"And there are no other papyri dealing with Ptahmes?"

"The one I translated—you read it that night in Egypt—is the only one I know of."

Carter spread his hands wide. "Then that leaves us exactly back at where we started—"

"Not necessarily," May said in a calm voice. "I'm sure you have heard how my father obtained various papyri."

"Well, there are... rumors..." Carter stammered.

"Please, there is no need to be polite." May stood, gathered all the papers on the table and tossed them into the fireplace to burn as she continued. "I have heard all the stories, I assure you. I'll have Matthews summon a cab to take you home to freshen up. I'll call on you in one hour,"—she turned to smile at him—"and you shall firsthand see if those stories have any basis in fact."

CHAPTER THIRTEEN

Precisely one hour later, Carter stepped into the taxi waiting in front of his house. May had changed into a crisp, business-like outfit.

"You look smashing..." Carter blurted out. "I mean, it fits you well... I mean, well, that's an attractive dress."

A small smile graced May's lips as she glanced at him, with a shy expression he had never seen from her before. "I'm happy you enjoy it," she said softly. "I chose it just for you."

Carter gave an embarrassed chuckle.

"Did you have any mysterious callers last night, as you predicted?" she continued in a matter-of-fact tone.

Carter grinned. "Yes, I had visitors. It was fortunate they were not too terribly messy."

"That's good to hear."

The cab maneuvered through traffic, stopping on Charing Cross Road. Four- and five-story masonry buildings, with fancy wedding cake structures of pillars and copulas loomed over the narrow street. Bookstores lined the first floors, their stock overflowing onto the crowded sidewalks. Browsers clustered around the low shelves, loaded with books with bright, colored spines, eager to find that one volume they needed.

Carter and May got out of the taxi. May led the way as they walked a couple of blocks down the sidewalk before turning off on a slender side lane. She stopped in front of a storefront marked by a painted sign over the shop window and door: M. Rudolf, Bookseller. Rare and Antiquarian Books.

The old bell above the door rang out with a dusty, muffled noise as the two stepped inside. The bookshelves lined every inch of wall space and most of the floor as well, rising like tall mountain ranges of tomes. Volumes of all shapes and sizes overflowed each one, their weight causing the shelves to sag under the strain. A well-dressed middle-aged woman stood in front of one shelf, browsing the titles.

"Mr. Rudolf?" May called.

"I shall be with you in one moment." A raspy voice, tinged by an Eastern European accent and sounding as dusty as the shop, came from behind a curtained doorway. In a second, Mr. Rudolf pushed his way through the drapes, a thick book held in one hand.

He was about five and a half feet tall, with a somewhat stocky and stout build. His eyes were large and bulging, like two hardboiled eggs. His black hair was slicked back, a stark contrast to his pallid skin. "Ah, Miss Ottley! A pleasure to see you again! I have recently acquired some interesting volumes on Egypt. Please browse while I finish with this customer."

May took Carter down a tight aisle. He cast a nervous eye at the towering bookcases, wondering how long it would take to dig them out if any one of the shelves collapsed and buried alive them in an avalanche of words.

Mr. Rudolf finished his business with the woman, the clang of a cash register and the tinkling of the bell over the door announcing the close of the transaction. He soon glided up to May and Carter, wearing the solicitous smile of a shark. "I understand Sir Robert had been taken ill."

"That is true," May said.

"And his condition...?" Mr. Rudolf cocked his head.

"There has been no change."

"That is most unfortunate." The bookseller clasped his hands in front of him. "Did you find any titles of interest?"

"As usual, you have many intriguing volumes,"—May glanced around at all the books—"but in truth, Mr. Rudolf, I'm seeking something older."

"Older?" One of Mr. Rudolf's eyebrows shot up.

"Yes. One might even say ancient."

The bookseller's eyes darted to Carter.

May made a small gesture toward Carter with one hand. "I can vouch for Mr. Pinsent. He is trustworthy."

Mr. Rudolf gave a slight bow and scuttled out of view. The front door locked, and in a moment, the bookseller returned. "Do you have anything particular in mind?"

"I rather fancy something more from the Hill of Rakh region." May sounded as though she were ordering off a restaurant menu. "If you have something available."

"Was that not the location of Sir Robert's last expedition?" A note of suspicion colored Mr. Rudolf's tone.

"It was," May replied with not an ounce of emotion showing through. "Discovered through... information obtained from you approximately three years ago."

"Ah, yes." Mr. Rudolf nodded. "I believe I have a clear recollection of the details of that transaction."

There was a long silence. Carter stood fascinated, a spectator of a high-stakes chess match played by two masterminds, each move calculated and strategic.

"It is quite interesting, this business," the bookseller went on, as though speaking about a different topic altogether. "Sometimes texts on a particular subject sit on the shelves for years, ignored, only to have more than one person inquire after them in a short time."

"That is most extraordinary, is it not?" With the skill of a magician, May withdrew a banknote from her purse and held it discreetly between her and Mr. Rudolf. His eyes flicked down at the bill, then, with the slightest of movements, he took it and slipped it into his pocket.

"As an odd coincidence, one interested party came into my shop a mere two hours ago," Mr. Rudolf said, "inquiring about a similar subject."

Carter stiffened. May did not appear to react.

"My, how quite unusual." May could have been speaking about the weather. "Were you able to fulfill his request?"

Mr. Rudolf shook his head sadly. "Sadly, no. I had nothing in stock that met his requirements."

"At all?"

"At this time."

"At this time," May emphasized. "Can I take it you did have something available previously?"

Mr. Rudolf did not respond, but only smiled back.

"Isn't that the way it always happens, Mr. Pinsent?" May asked lightly. "As soon as you decide to purchase something, it is sold to another customer." She regarded the bookseller for a moment. "It is possible I could be interested in the same item. If so, perhaps this buyer and I could come to an understanding to our mutual benefit. What is his name?"

"Miss Ottley, I'm sure you understand that I don't divulge information on those who patronize my establishment." Mr. Rudolf spread his hands in apology.

Another note appeared from May's purse and vanished into Mr. Rudolf's pocket.

"You have learned well from Sir Robert," Mr. Rudolf complimented. "Permit me one moment, if you will be so kind."

The bookseller disappeared. There was the ring of the cash register, then he returned, holding a slip of paper in his hand. He handed it to May. She tucked it in her handbag without looking at it.

"Thank you very much for your assistance, Mr. Rudolf," May said. "As always, it is a pleasure conducting business with you."

"As with you, Miss Ottley." Mr. Rudolf bowed his head and stepped to one side. "Please do come again."

"I will, of course."

Mr. Rudolf turned to Carter. "And you as well, Mr. Pinsent. Do come back. I have an extensive selection of stimulating materials and photographs a young man such as you would be sure to enjoy."

"Thank you," Carter said, a little unsure on how to respond.

May began to walk past the bookseller then stopped. "Oh, Mr. Rudolf, perhaps you can provide one last thing, given the generosity of the commission on this transaction. The customer who came in earlier... did you give the same information to him?"

The bookseller scowled as though smelling a rotten egg. "No. I do not care for him."

"Who was he? I think I may know him."

Mr. Rudolf smiled. "I believe you do. It was Dr. William Belleville."

Carter and May emerged from the shop, blinking as their eyes adjusted to the midday sun. Carter breathed in the fresh air. Despite his love for books and their company, being tucked away among shelves in the tiny store almost reminded him of when he was stuffed in that coffin. He relished the warmth of sunshine on his face.

He turned to May in admiration. "I've never viewed a performance like that in my life."

"Thank you. As Mr. Rudolf said, I learned from a master," May said with a touch of pride.

"I guess so," Carter said. He leaned forward with eager anticipation. "Well? What's on that paper?"

"First, let us take a spot of tea at the Savoy, and we'll examine it," she said her crisp way, "then we shall plan our next steps."

It took longer to be seated than the actual trip to the hotel itself. May seemed to be acquainted with every other person in the tearoom, requiring quick conversations at various tables. After completing a voyage around the room, they took their seats. May gave their orders, then pulled out the note Mr. Rudolf had written.

"That stands to reason." She sighed after she glanced at what was written on the note. She passed it to Carter.

"Caspian Greenwood," he read out loud. He handed the paper back to May. "I've heard of him. Made millions of pounds selling munitions, and he's not too selective about who his customers are if they can meet his price. He's also one of the largest private collectors of Egyptian artifacts in the country."

"In the world, perhaps. And large in many ways," she said as she slipped the paper to her purse. "He and my father have clashed frequently... at auctions, for sales from various sources... and personally."

"And you think Mr. Rudolf sold him the papyrus we need?" Carter asked, then he shrugged. "Although I must admit, I couldn't follow what you two were talking about. You seemed to be speaking in code."

May laughed. "My father and I have dealt with Mr. Rudolf for years, so we understand each other." She sipped her tea, then smiled and waved at an older woman at another table. "Based on what I gleaned from Mr. Rudolf, I believe Mr. Greenwood does have possession of it. His reaction to us will be most interesting."

CHAPTER FOURTEEN

The building was no different from its neighbors on the narrow street: grimy, with dirty windows and doors. Pushcarts jostled with trucks for space on the pavement while men, yelling orders to each other, pushed dollies stacked high with crates in and out of the various warehouses.

"Are you sure this is the correct address, miss?" The cabbie turned back over the seat.

"Oh, yes, absolutely, driver," May replied as she handed him some bills. "I do not require change."

The driver's eyes bulged out at the amount of money in his hand. He tugged at the brim of his cap. "Of course, miss. Thank you, miss."

"Come, Carter." May stepped out of the taxi, followed by Carter.

"Is this where Mr. Greenwood stores his collection?" Carter asked, gazing over the warehouse-like building.

"Not only that, he lives here with it," May said.

Carter looked around at the surroundings in disbelief. "Here?"

May nodded as they arrived at a nondescript metal door that blended into the surrounding brick. She pressed the discreet button beside it, and they waited. After a number of minutes, a small slot slid aside near the top of the door, revealing a pair of eyes staring out from the darkness on the other side.

"Miss Ottley to see Mr. Greenwood," May stated.

The eyes on the other side of the opening narrowed.

She waved toward Carter in answer to the unspoken question. "This is my bodyguard."

Carter managed to contain his surprise at his new assigned role. The slot closed, then came the sound of several locks snapping open. The door swung wide. May strode inside, with Carter following the appropriate few steps behind.

They entered a dim hallway. A massive figure stood by the door, stuffed into a butler's uniform that failed to hide the fact the wearer more properly belonged in a boxing ring. His heavy-lidded eyes appraised Carter, and his lips tightened in an expression that could have been a smile or a sneer. The man was at least twice Carter's size, and although Carter tried to meet him with a hard stare of his own, deep down he knew this man could break him in two over his knee like a broomstick.

The butler closed the door and led the two down the dank hallway, opening a set of double doors at the far end. He stood to one side as Carter and May stepped through. A gasp escaped Carter's lips.

The center of the warehouse was open, soaring four stories to a glass, conservatory-style roof. A huge granite statue of a seated

Pharaoh Ramesses II dominated the middle of the space. Another colossal statue of Pharaoh Amenhotep III was nearby. Several panels from tombs hung on one wall, painted with images of life after death, telling tales of the dead kings' glorious journeys through the underworld to an eternal paradise called the Field of Reeds. Fragments of friezes dotted another one—scenes depicting royalty hunting animals or worshiping gods, reinforcing generations of Egyptians' belief that even the hereafter was dictated by one's earthly deeds. Along all the walls were spotted sarcophagi decorated in striking detail standing upright on edge like soldiers on guards' duty.

Cabinets displayed funerary figurines, picturesque portrayals of people kneeling before boats ferrying them over the waters of the underworld on their journey to eternity, as well as delicate statues and jewelry box lids painted with beautiful illustrations of everyday utensils such as combs and mirrors. More showcases held pottery, metalwork and exquisite necklaces.

Carter was still trying to take in the size and quality of the collection when a voice interrupted: "Thank you, Jack. That is all." He turned toward the source.

Mr. Caspian Greenwood walked in their direction. The man was enormous—at least twenty stone—with the largest gut Carter had ever seen on a human. But that was where most of the weight seemed to lie. While he wore his double chin like a sash across his face, it wasn't muzzled with fat. His head was bald, and his black eyes were matched by black eyebrows, the only slash of color on a pale canvas. He had on Turkish slippers, black pants, a light blue silk shirt and an elaborately embroidered smoking jacket.

"Miss Ottley, what a surprise to see you." Mr. Greenwood's voice was deep but had a hollow sound as though it emerged from a tomb.

"Mr. Greenwood." May flashed a tight smile. "This is Carter, my bodyguard."

"Bodyguard?" Mr. Greenwood cast a glance toward Carter.

Carter widened his stance, put on a grim expression, and crossed his arms in a way he hoped made his biceps bulge under his suit coat.

"Yes," May said. "After all, you do not live in a particularly safe section of the city."

Mr. Greenwood chuckled. It sounded more like a series of grunts than laughter. "I find that prevents unwanted guests. Which reminds me, how is Sir Robert?"

"Unfortunately, my father is at present in the hospital," May said.

"Oh, how dreadful. I am sorry," Mr. Greenwood said.

No, you're not, Carter thought.

"So what do I owe the honor of a visit from you?" Mr. Greenwood asked.

"I have a business proposition I wish to discuss with you," May said.

Mr. Greenwood's right eyebrow shot up. "Really? You never struck me as one to become involved arming revolutionaries in far-flung South American countries."

May returned a polite party laugh. "That business I leave to you. I wish to talk about another matter."

"Well, I must say I'm intrigued. Let us continue in a civilized manner." Mr. Greenwood bowed and gestured toward an open door. "Your... bodyguard may come as well."

"Thank you. You may speak without concern in front of him. Carter," May directed. She may as well have been ordering a dog to heel.

Carter trailed behind May and Mr. Greenwood, passing display case after display case holding the most stunning and remarkable artifacts he'd ever seen.

Four floors containing windows overlooking the atrium rose at the far end of the warehouse, which Carter supposed must contain Mr. Greenwood's living quarters. The three passed through an entry door, as elegant as any London mansion, into a wood-paneled hall. A carved staircase hugged an ornately designed elevator, and polished marble tiles made up the floor. Two large oil paintings depicting Egypt adorned the walls.

Carter and May's host led them into a cozy, paneled drawing room, entering through double doors that opened without a sound. Their feet sank into the thick Oriental rug spread on the floor. On their left, windows looked out onto an atrium, and in the center of the opposite wall, a fire burned in the black-marbled fireplace. Flanking the mantle were shelves, holding more ancient Egyptian pottery. The furniture was made of dark woods, highlighted by gold leaf and featuring ornate carvings of hieroglyphics, lotus flowers and sphinxes. The upholstery was richly colored.

Mr. Greenwood waved toward a sofa. "Please be seated, Miss Ottley."

Carter realized as a servant, he was meant to stand. As May sat, Mr. Greenwood settled his bulk into a wing chair while Carter took up a position by the double doors.

"Now, then," —Mr. Greenwood tented his fingers—"what is the business matter you mentioned?"

"I would like to purchase an item I believe you own," May proposed.

Mr. Greenwood chuckled. "Young lady, I am sure you are well aware I acquire objects *for* my collection, not to offer them for sale. I am not a common merchant."

"Not a common one at all, but I hoped you might make an exception in my case."

Mr. Greenwood pulled a cigar out of a silver box sitting on a table next to him. "What is this object you wish to purchase... and I will not sell you?"

May met Mr. Greenwood's gaze. "A papyrus."

"That is rather a vague description," Mr. Greenwood dismissed as he lit his cigar.

"Allow me to be more specific, then. The one I have in mind is from the Hill of Rakh region." May leaned back on the sofa.

Mr. Greenwood stared at May expressionless, rolling the cigar in his mouth. He removed it and blew out a cloud of blue gray smoke. "It appears you have been speaking with our mutual friend, Mr. Rudolf."

"It cost me dearly."

"No doubt. Conversations with him can become quite costly." Mr. Greenwood tapped some cigar ash into a crystal ashtray.

"My father has been investigating a tomb in that area," May said. "The papyrus is necessary for that work."

Mr. Greenwood grinned. "I am well aware of that fact."

May sat up straight. "I am prepared to pay five hundred pounds for the object."

"I'm afraid I must decline your offer." The collector returned the cigar to his mouth.

"One thousand pounds," May said.

"That is a very attractive sum indeed, but again, alas, I must say no. The item in question is not for sale." Mr. Greenwood puffed on his cigar. He chuckled. "At any price. Even to such a gracious young lady as yourself."

Mary took a deep breath. "Mr. Greenwood, the papyrus may be vital to my father's recovery."

"My regrets."

The uneasy negotiations between the two sides had reached a stalemate. Carter decided to try and break the stand-off with his own hands. Literally. Without a word, he sauntered towards a set of shelves. He stopped in front of one and surveyed the contents.

"Stay away from those, young man," Mr. Greenwood rapped. "Those objects are priceless."

Carter picked up an Egyptian painted pottery jar. He put on his best impression of a Cockney accent. "Be a bleedin' shame if I dropped this, eh guv'nor?"

Mr. Greenwood leaned forward in his chair, his eyes narrowing to angry slits. He aimed his cigar at Carter. "Return that item. I can summon Jack, and when he's finished with you, sirrah, they'll have to scrape you off the floor with a spoon."

Carter grinned. "Cor blimey, that might be true, but I can give things a right ol' bash before it comes to that, mate!"

May stood and put down her purse. "And I will assist Carter. If that is what it takes to make you reasonable."

Mr. Greenwood swung around to face May, surprised.

"I reckon me mistress's offer of two 'undred fifty quid is well decent," Carter said. "'Specially for some bleedin' ancient bit of paper, innit?"

"Two hundred and fifty!" Mr. Greenwood thundered.

Carter held the jar arm's length over the floor. "I'd snap it up, I would."

Mr. Greenwood blustered, blowing his checks in and out a few times like a fish. After looking back and forth between the two, he bowed his head to Carter. "I concede defeat. Kindly replace that artifact."

"Hold on a sec, mate. Give that there paper to me mistress afore anythin' else." Carter hoisted the jar over his head.

The collector chuckled as he stood up from his chair. "Gad, you're a character, sirrah, a character." Shuffling over to the sideboard between the windows, he opened a drawer and extracted a cloth sack. He handed the bag to May, who peered inside. She nodded to Carter.

"We appreciate your assistance, Mr. Greenwood," she said pleasantly. She sat down, and then retrieved a pen and check from her purse. After scribbling something on it, she gave the paper to Mr. Greenwood.

The collector glanced at the check and stuffed it into a pocket of his smoking jacket. He faced Carter. "And now, sirrah, please replace that object to where it belongs. With great care."

"'Course, mate." Carter placed the jar on the shelf. He jerked his thumb toward it. "It's a lovely piece, that. Me guess it's New Kingdom, Late Dynasty. I'd wager 'round 1300 B.C."

Mr. Greenwood's mouth was half-open and his eyes wide as Carter walked back to the room's entrance, but he had composed himself by the time May joined Carter at the double doors.

"Thank you again for your cooperation, Mr. Greenwood," May said. "I greatly appreciate it."

Mr. Greenwood's lips curled into a sinister smile. His icy glare bore into Carter, and his voice was laced with venom as he spoke: "My pleasure, Miss Ottley. And to you, young man, I swear—if you ever dare cross my threshold again, I shall order Jack to tear you limb from limb."

Carter took May by the elbow and guided her out of the room. They hurried past Mr. Greenwood's immense collection of ancient artifacts without giving them more than a passing glance. Carter regretted not having more time to take in the beauty of those pieces, but he was positive that would not be welcomed, not to mention Jack's hulking presence to the back of them. The two left the warehouse, Jack slamming the door behind them. Locks clicked into place.

May turned to Carter. "That was brilliant."

Carter tapped two fingers to his forehead. "Ta muchly, miss. I really appreciate that, I do."

May giggled. "Where did you learn to speak like that?"

"From Burt. He's one of the porters at my school," Carter grinned. "I told you I inherited my mother's skills for languages. Dialects, too." He looked around to get his bearings. "Aldgate East tube station should be this way."

The two started walking down the street.

"Are you sure that is the correct papyrus?" Carter pointed to the bag May held.

"Yes. Mr. Rudolf's inventory tag is still on it," she said.

"Let's get back to your house." Carter said. "We need to translate the papyrus as soon as possible. The time for our fathers is running out."

After a few blocks, Carter got the same uncomfortable feeling he had in Port Said. He glanced over his shoulder, then took hold of May's arm. "In here," he said under his breath, guiding her into a newsagent's shop.

"What is it?" she asked.

"We're being followed," Carter said in a low voice.

"How do you know?"

"Experience," Carter replied grimly. "Give me the papyrus, quick."

May did so. Carter pulled it out of the bag, unrolled it, taking a rapid glance at it. "It's not very complicated. It looks more like a list." He tore it in two.

"What are you doing?" May gasped.

"Insurance, and bargaining power," Carter answered as he handed one half back to May. He slipped his part into the latest issue of *Tatler* magazine he took off the rack. "One part is worthless without the other."

The shopkeeper came through some curtains in the rear of the small shop. Carter paid for the magazine, then he and May left.

"Where are those—" May started to say.

"Don't look! We don't want them to know we've caught on to them." Carter cautioned. "It's two young blokes, about our age, about half a block in back. Let's keep going."

The pair continued to stroll up the street.

"I want you to take the first cab you see," Carter said. "I'll continue on to the Underground station. They'll have to split up to follow us, or more likely they'll just stay on my trail. With my red hair, I'm probably easier to track. I'll lose them on the Tube, then meet you at the British Museum refreshment room in two hours."

"Here's one."

Carter hailed it. When the taxi pulled up, he opened the door for May. She climbed in.

"Good luck." She kissed him on the cheek.

Blood rushed to Carter's face. He smiled. "I'll see you in two hours."

"Refreshment room, British Museum." She closed the cab door.

As the cab drove away, Carter glanced at his watch and out of the corner of his eye saw his trackers were still there. The boys wore caps rakishly tilted on their heads, patterned shirts and vests with black pants that ended in scuffed boots. The only bright spot on their outfits was the garishly colored neckerchiefs tied around their necks.

Carter maintained a steady pace, his mind in turmoil. Part of him now wished he had left the papyrus alone. If he hadn't torn it in half, May would still have the whole document with her in the taxi. The two blokes tailing him may decide to drop the pursuit and turn to robbery. But at the same time, what if there were more people tracking them than just those two behind him? Could someone be also following May at this moment? He wondered if he had made a mistake and they should have stayed together instead.

He picked up his pace as he entered the squat, stone Aldgate East tube station, hurrying to the booking hall and buying a ticket to King's Cross railway station. Carter reached the platform just as the train pulled in. He congratulated himself when he thought he'd lost his pursuers. But moments later, the young men in bright neckerchiefs appeared as well.

Carter boarded a crowded carriage, while the other two hopped on another. King's Cross was London's biggest and busiest railway terminus, which gave him hope that he could lose his tails in the mob there. Then he planned to circle back to the Underground.

Three different lines went through it, so even if they guessed he'd gone back to the tube, they wouldn't know which one he took.

The train pulled into King's Cross; Carter sprang out of his seat and charged forward, pushing past the other passengers like a bull. He muttered apologies about being late for a departure as he darted out of the door. Sprinting to the railway platforms, dodging and weaving, he slipped through the other travelers with sharp turns and leaps.

When he reached the main concourse, stunning with its overarching glass roof supported by ornate iron posts, some luck came his way. Another man, about his height and with red hair, was walking toward the platforms, surrounded by other people so his clothes weren't visible.

Let those blokes follow him, Carter thought as he gave a short laugh of triumph. He made a sudden turn, to the great annoyance of a group following him. He dashed off a hurried "sorry" and darted out of King's Cross, crossed Pancras Street, and went into St. Pancras Station. He slowed his pace and checked behind him. His followers were nowhere in sight.

Carter grinned at his success as entered the Underground and purchased his ticket. He rode around the Underground in an aimless pattern for an hour and a half, changing lines several times until he finally arrived at the British Museum stop. Walking quickly to the refreshment room, he made his way to an empty table in the corner, sat facing the door and ordered himself a hot cup of tea. He transferred the papyrus to his inside coat pocket and leafed through the magazine.

He had just taken his first sip from his second cup when a dirty and disheveled young street urchin, no older than twelve, walked in. The other visitors pulled away from the boy as he passed, almost as if he had something contagious. He scanned the room then went straight for Carter's table.

The lad held out a creamy white folded note, a stark contrast to his filthy hands. "'Scuse me, guv'nor, a lady requested I give this to ya."

Carter took the paper. "Who was this lady?"

"Dunno, mate. She just told me to pass this on to ya, she did." He drew the back of one hand across his runny nose.

"Thank you." Carter reached into his pocket and fished out some coins. He gave them to the urchin.

The boy's eyes opened wide at the money. "Blimey, guv'nor. That's right decent of ya. Cheers!" He ran from the room.

Carter unfolded the message with trembling hands. He recognized May's handwriting: "Carter: London Docks. Come at once. Imperative. M."

He set off immediately and it was late afternoon when he arrived at St. Katharine Docks, a group of multistorey, dirty warehouses clustered on the banks of the Thames River, as gloomy as the nearby Tower of London. Dirt coated the surface of each building and blackened the windows. Steam hissed from inside some of the structures, and the sour stench of some long-ago forgotten spilled cargo filled the air. Thumps and clangs of moving crates bounced through the leaden atmosphere.

The dockworkers ignored him as he trudged along the murky Thames. He crossed the small drawbridge at St. Katharine Docks and reached the London Docks. There was no sign of May. His gut began to twist as he looked around and thought about the message she sent him, wondering how he'd find her if she was concealing herself somewhere nearby. Carter passed a young man sitting on a crate near the entrance to an alley that ran between two warehouses.

"Y'looking for a bird, mate?" he asked.

Carter stopped.

"I says, you on the lookout for a lady, mate?" The young man took a drag on his cigarette. "The one who dropped ya that note?"

"Yes," Carter answered warily.

The ruffian jerked his head toward the alley. "Down there, guv."

Carter hesitated, his eyes narrowing in suspicion.

The young man flicked off some cigarette ash in a bored way. "Better leg it if ya wanna find her all in one piece. Afore the blokes 'ave a pop at 'er."

Carter burned with anger. "They bloody well better keep their filthy hands off her."

He charged down the alleyway, chased by the young man's mocking laugh, emerging on a dock with the Thames lapping against it. Somebody jumped him from the rear. He stumbled forward and shook off his opponent. Spinning around, he planted a fist into the man's face. It was one of the blokes that had followed him earlier. Several other teens swarmed from the shadows of the dockside like rats.

The heat of rage steamed inside Carter as he unleashed a fierce barrage of punches. But it was too little, too late. He was outnumbered and outmatched. Two assailants grabbed hold of him, pinning his arms behind his back. The first attacker stalked closer to Carter like an animal, nostrils flared, panting and wiping some blood from his mouth.

"You can look after yerself, mate, I'd say that. I'd fancy wrappin' this up, but I've got me marching orders, see." The young man pawed through Carter's jacket and took out the papyrus. He addressed the other boys. "Give 'im a dip in the drink, lads."

Carter's feet dragged along the dockside as the two teens shoved him forward. He thrashed and bucked in an attempt to free himself as they reached the edge of the pier. With a sudden violent pivot, he threw off the two holding him. He spun around and pulled back his fist.

He barely had time to recognize the heavy timber swung at his face before it smacked into his forehead. He toppled backward, pitching into the murky depths of the Thames, his body sinking deeper and deeper, until all light faded away.

CHAPTER FIFTEEN

The icy embrace of the Thames clutched Carter as he sank deeper and deeper. He thrashed wildly, desperate to return to the air. The filthy murk of the water smothered him, no matter how much he fought. His lungs were about to burst from aching for oxygen. His limbs ached as he kicked and clawed in search of a way up top, but only liquid blackness swirled about him.

Just when he thought his time had come, his head broke the surface. Flailing at first, he finally began to tread water. He gasped for air, spitting out the putrid river before inhaling huge gulps. His fight with the current made him weak and he was numb from the icy water surrounding him.

The river had carried him some distance downstream from where he had originally gone in. Blinking away the stinging water, he spotted some wharves reaching into the river, a single gas lamp burning on one end.

He struck out for the pier. Eddies lapped around him, tearing at his clothes and sucking away the strength in his limbs. At last, his fingers grazed against a ladder that descended from the wharf.

He hugged the wooden plank rungs with both hands like a sailor clinging to a mast in a storm, refusing to let go no matter how hard the current yanked. The Thames would not take him as its prize.

Pausing for a few minutes to rest, he glanced up the ladder. It seemed to stretch on endlessly to the starry sky above. Steeling himself, he slowly began his climb up the ladder, not daring to look up and see how much farther there was to go. He remained focused and repeated the same motions of shifting his hands and feet one more rung at a time. Again. And again. And again.

Carter dragged his body over the edge of the wharf and sprawled on the splintery wooden boards, his lungs heaving with exertion. He coughed and spat out mouthfuls of the dirty river water, gasping for air as he got up to his hands and knees. A voice—deep, rich and trained—spoke out of the night.

"'Full fathom five thy father lies; Of his bones are coral made; Those are pearls that were his eyes: Nothing of him that doth fade, But doth suffer a sea-change into something rich and strange.'"

A figure lounged on a crate next to the gas lamp a few feet away, puffing on a pipe. He reminded Carter of Father Christmas—rotund, with a white beard and equally white, wild hair sticking out from under a brown hat. His eyes were kind, but his face was sad. The man wore a large, formless white shirt. His pants were blue denim, mended in a dozen places by thread showing brown through the worn cloth. The boots were scuffed with much use.

Carter wiped his mouth with the back of his hand and tried to stand, but his legs gave out and he stumbled back down onto his knees. "Who are you?" he said, his voice weak and raspy.

The man raised his bulk with a groan. "A friend, young man, of which you appear to be in great need right about now." He walked heavily over to Carter and helped him to his feet. "My humble lodgings are less than a block away. Are you able to traverse the distance? I would provide a ride on my cart, but, as you can observe, it is laden with wonderful treasures."

He waved one hand toward a nearby pushcart, loaded with rags, bottles, paper, empty containers of all sorts and pieces of metal. "As you might surmise, my dear sir, my current occupation is what is in the vernacular called a 'ragpicker'. But that was not always the case, young man, not always the case." He threw one arm wide and declaimed, "'When I was at home, I was in a better place: but travelers must be content.'"

In spite of his situation, Carter grinned. "I would be most grateful of your help, sir."

"Splendid, young man, splendid! I shall delight with your company!" The man hoisted the handles of the handcart. "'Once more, dear friends, unto the breach!'"

The pair started down the street, the man huffing like a steam engine at the exertion of pushing the full cart. Guilty at only walking alongside, Carter relieved the man of one of the pushcart's handles. The man nodded his thanks between wheezes.

Soon they turned down a narrow lane. Brick buildings, as wide as they were tall, rose on either side of the cobbled street. The road passed a small house that had somehow survived from the 1700s. A half-timbered building, two stories high and spindly, with diamond-paned windows. The wood had weathered to a dark mahogany, the plaster dirty and gray. Piping along the outside indicated it had been modernized at one point with indoor plumbing.

They entered the house's tiny rear garden. It was almost full of the same type of objects in the man's pushcart.

"This is fine." The man stopped the cart with a grateful moan. "I shall unload tomorrow. Now, we must get you out of those wet clothes."

He led Carter inside the house. Stacks of items hugging one wall made the narrow hallway even tighter. Unlike the back garden, these piles were tidy and well-organized, layer upon layer of curiosities reaching all the way to the ceiling.

"Excuse my merchandise, young man," the man said, gesturing to the stacks. "The parlor is at the front."

That room was as clogged as the hall, but with piles of books and magazines lining the walls. The room was a controlled mess, but enough open floor space remained for a well-worn, comfortable chair and settee facing the fireplace. Flames crackled in the hearth.

"Remove your clothes and set them by the fire to dry," the man said as he turned up the gas light. "I will endeavor to find something else for you to wear. I keep my clothing stock in the dining room."

The man left the room, and Carter thankfully peeled off his soaking garments. He laid them on the fire screen in front of the mantle. As he stood closer to the fire to warm himself, Carter noticed a volume sitting on the repaired side table next to the armchair. It was thick and bound with an aged leather cover.

Wondering why that book wasn't buried in a stack with all the others, he opened it and saw it was a complete collection of William Shakespeare's plays.

Carter started flipping through the pages, noticing inked comments in the margins, crossed out lines and diagrams showing how the words should be spoken. This wasn't meant as a simple reading copy; someone had been working on this text.

"'Our revels now are ended.'" The ragpicker stood in the door, holding some clothes in one hand. He continued in a sad, quiet voice, the lament of a person who had lost something dear. His eyes were not focused on the small room, but beyond it, into the past. "'These our actors, as I foretold you, were all spirits, and are melted into air, into thin air; And, like the baseless fabric of this vision, the cloud-capp'd towers, the gorgeous palaces, the solemn temples, the great globe itself, yea, all which it inherit, shall dissolve; And, like this insubstantial pageant faded, leave not a rack behind. We are such stuff as dreams are made on, and our little life is rounded with a sleep.'"

Carter stood in an awkward silence for a moment. He closed the volume. "I'm sorry. I didn't mean to pry. The book was lying here, and I was curious..."

The man's eyes cleared of the mist and they fixed on Carter. He smiled. "It is not necessary to apologize, young man." He held out a pair of overalls, a blue-striped shirt and cap. "These should fit you."

"Thank you." Carter took the clothes and dressed.

"Now you are clothed, allow me to introduce myself formally." The man stood erect and proud. "I am Kenton Buckingham, proclaimed by many reviewers to be the finest interpreter of William Shakespeare in our lifetime." He pulled a cameo out of his pocket and gazed at it. "Along with my exquisite late wife Lenore, we toured the provinces, enacting the works of the immortal bard to throngs of spellbound audience members. Ah, the applause! The cheers! Bravo! Bravo!" He grinned at the memories and handed the small portrait to Carter as though it was a priceless diamond. "Lenore as she appeared in her crowning role of Juliet."

Carter held the picture in his hands and stared at it. The woman was beautiful, with long black hair and porcelain skin, which glowed like moonlight. Her intelligent eyes sparkled like stars. He gave the cameo back the Kenton. "She's lovely."

Kenton took the image, stroking it with one of his thumbs. "That she was, young man, that she was. 'My love is thine to teach. Teach it but how, and thou shalt see how apt it is to learn to grime in gentle arts,'" he whispered to the engraved image. He tenderly kissed it before replacing it in his pocket. "Cruel fate snatched her from me and this world. Then liquor drowned the pain of her loss... but also the glittering, magical world of the footlights."

He sat in the chair and gestured for Carter to sit. He pounded one arm and exclaimed in pride. "But I beat down the evil demon from the bottle, sir! I imagined what my lovely Lenore would think of me if she encountered me in such a sad and disreputable state. Alas, by then my reputation as a reliable thespian was in tatters."

Carter took the seat. "I'm sorry about your wife, and your professional difficulties. Perhaps someday you'll…"

Kenton waved off the sentiment. He reached for a pipe from a small rack resting behind the book of Shakespeare. A grinning pottery skull, a crack running down one side, sat next to it. Kenton removed the skull cap, took out some tobacco and filled the bowl. "Although I would dearly love to tread the boards again, I do not put my faith in dreams or horoscopes. Or actor managers. Well, sir, you know who I am, but I do not know who is sharing the warmth of my fire. It seems not an equitable trade, now does it?"

Carter smiled. "No, it doesn't. Carter Pinsent here. A pleasure to meet you, Mr. Buckingham."

Kenton inclined his head. "And you, Mr. Pinsent. Tell me, what brought you crawling out of the Thames like Ferdinand in 'The Tempest'?" He lit his pipe.

"A gang of toughs overwhelmed me near the London Docks and pitched me in the river," Carter said.

"A swarm of scurvy knaves, eh?" He puffed his pipe. The sweet scent of tobacco filled the air. "Were they thieves?"

"Yes."

"They set upon you at the London Docks, do you say?"

Carter nodded.

Kenton inspected Carter. "Odd. You do not appear to be the type of fellow to frequent such a locale, especially at night."

"I was stupid… I acted without thinking," Carter confessed. "I was led to believe I would meet… a certain young lady there."

Kenton leaned toward Carter and winked. "Your young lady?"

The question threw Carter. He had never really considered May in that way, but... He grinned sheepishly. "Yes."

"Ah! 'A pair of star-crossed lovers'!" Kenton spread his arms wide. "And you were meeting at an out of the way spot because your families...?"

"Our fathers don't get along," Carter admitted.

"Well, let us hope you two do not follow the tragic path of 'Romeo and Juliet'," Kenton said.

"True." Carter stood. "I thank you for your assistance, but I must—"

Kenton got up. "No, no, no! I won't hear of you leaving, young Carter! Look out the window! It is night. You have already encountered one pack of ruffians today. You'd be sure to meet another one as you try to make your way out of this district in the dark. While you are built well, I am positive you do not wish to repeat your experience again."

"I can take care of myself," Carter declared.

"As you so aptly demonstrated earlier tonight?"

"Well, that was different..." Carter sputtered. "There were too many of them... they... they jumped me from behind... and... look... they hit me with a stick..." Kenton continued to stare at him, puffing on his pipe. "And... and..." Carter gave up.

"Besides," Kenton said, "what progress can you make ascertaining your young lady's whereabouts tonight?"

The obvious thought of going to the police crossed Carter's mind, but he dismissed it. They would never be able to find May in a city of four million. More likely than not, by now she had fallen under the control of Dr. Belleville, who must have realized the papyrus was incomplete. Now he had Carter's part as well and required May's knowledge to decipher it. That kept her safe—for now, at least. Beyond that, there was nothing Carter could do.

"You're right," he said after a pause. He sank onto the settee. "And I do admit, I am exhausted."

"It's settled, then!" Kenton clapped his hands together in satisfaction. "That settee is not particularly comfortable, but is more so than the many train seats I've had to use as beds, rushing from one engagement to another. In the morning, I will prepare a repast to dispatch you on your quest with a full stomach."

"I thank you for your hospitality," Carter said gratefully.

"'Tis but nothing!" Kenton performed a deep, sweeping Elizabethan bow. "'Good night, and better health attend his majesty!'"

Carter grinned as Kenton left the room. He punched the cushions of the settee. Making himself as comfortable as possible, he dropped off to sleep.

The breakfast was the most enjoyable Carter had had in several years, letting him forget his worries for a moment. He watched his host in awe, entranced by his energy and skill.

Kenton moved about the tiny kitchen with fluid grace despite his large size, cracking the eggs into a bowl then whisking them with an intensity suggesting he was in character. While he cooked, the actor regaled Carter with tales of his glory days in the theater and recited soliloquies from Shakespearean plays.

After he served the meal, Kenton sat down, describing how he would stage various plays, popping sausage and egg into his mouth as he continued to speak without missing a beat. It was a feat which left Carter rather impressed. When breakfast finally ended, it felt like the curtain fell on a great performance that had him wanting more.

At the back door, Carter gripped Kenton's hand. "I cannot thank you enough for your kindness and hospitality."

"Please..." Kenton said with a smile and a modest tilt of his head.

"How can I repay you?"

"You're leaving your other clothes here. They will fetch me a pretty penny, young man," Kenton grinned. "That is payment enough."

"Can I come back and visit you again?" Carter asked shyly, almost afraid of a negative answer.

"By all means! Anytime, Carter, anytime!" Kenton said as though projecting to the back balcony. He tapped Carter on his shoulder. "And do bring your young lady along, as well."

Carter was ashamed May had slipped his mind during breakfast. He smiled. "Yes, of course, I'll bring her, too."

After another round of handshakes, Carter decided his best plan of action would be to set off towards May's house, although he was unsure of what he would discover. Would she be there? Did she make it to her home? Why didn't she meet him at the British Museum?

A disturbing thought came to him. Had May tricked him, luring him into a trap with her note so his portion of the papyrus could be stolen—and he be conveniently disposed of?

But why would she do that? Had she been working with Dr. Belleville all along? Or was she being held captive by the evil—for that is what Carter now considered him—doctor?

The questions swirled through Carter's head, fighting for dominance over his thoughts and emotions. He was so occupied with his thoughts he almost walked into traffic, jumping back on the sidewalk at the blare of a horn.

He glanced around, recognizing the familiar streets and landmarks leading to St. Bartholomew's. He detoured to the hospital, praying his father was out of danger and all this trouble with Dr. Belleville and the ancient papyri could be forgotten.

A spark of hope had remained in his heart, but now it was snuffed out. The doctor gravely informed him his father and Sir Robert's conditions had not changed. Both men still lay in an unknown form of suspended animation, wasting away from a lack of nourishment. They were also still in isolation due to the mysterious nature of their sickness. Although the doctor didn't say it, the prognosis wasn't good.

Carter left the hospital depressed. If he—with or without May's help—couldn't find a way to reverse the effects of the mysterious injection they believed Dr. Belleville had given to his father and Sir Robert, their fathers would die in less than two weeks. The only chance of finding an antidote was from the papyrus, but now it was gone... perhaps along with May too.

Four weary hours later, he finally reached May's house. His feet were heavy and his legs sore as he climbed the stone steps leading to the front door. He pounded the brass knocker, the dull thud reverberating inside. After a few moments, Matthews opened the door and took one disdainful look at Carter. The annoyance at the breach of etiquette his expression displayed was unmistakable.

"Tradesmen are to use the rear entrance," the butler sniffed, and began to shut the door.

"No, wait, Matthews, it's me." Carter took off his cap. "Carter Pinsent. Remember? I stayed over the other night."

"Oh, yes, Mr. Pinsent. I am sorry about the reception, but some tradespeople just don't seem to understand protocol." Matthews examined Carter. He added in an apology, "It's just the manner of your dress."

"It's a long story," Carter said. "Is May... Miss Ottley in?"

"I'm afraid not, sir."

"Oh." A thought jolted him: did she make it back in the cab at all? "Was she here yesterday?"

"Yesterday, sir?" Matthews asked, puzzled.

"Yes. It's important I know."

"Why, yes, sir, she was here yesterday. It was my day off, but the upstairs maid informed me of Miss Ottley being home," Matthews said.

"And she's not here now?" Carter moved to peer around the butler, as though he could spot May hiding in the hallway.

"I already told you that, sir. No, she is not." A note of irritation crept into Matthew's usually bland voice.

"When did she leave? Earlier today?" Carter pressed.

"I beg your pardon, sir, these questions are highly—" Matthews started to say.

"It's critical!" Carter shouted. He calmed down and continued in a more even tone. "I'm sorry. Did she leave yesterday or today?"

For a second, it seemed Matthews was going to refuse to answer, but instead he gave a resigned sigh. "Yesterday, sir. In the late afternoon or early evening, according to the maid."

"When do you expect her to return?" Carter asked.

"I really do not know, sir," Matthews answered. "You see, sir, Miss Ottley has left the country."

CHAPTER SIXTEEN

"**L**eft the country!" It took a moment for Carter to recover from the surprise. "Where? Do you know?"

"The south of France, I believe, sir," Matthews replied.

"The south of France..." Carter mumbled to himself. There was something wrong with that answer, but he couldn't quite place what. He looked at the butler. "Why? Did she give a reason?"

"Sir, I sincerely do not think—"

"Did she say why she went to the south of France?" Carter yelled in frustration. He held up both hands and took a deep breath. Anger wouldn't get him anywhere. He continued in a quieter tone. "I apologize for shouting. It's that she and I had an engagement planned, and she did not appear. I am concerned if anything has happened to her, that is all."

Matthews permitted himself a slight, knowing smile. "I understand, sir."

No, you don't, you smug... Carter thought. He went on in as calm a way as he could muster. "Did Miss Ottley give any reason for this sudden trip?"

"No, sir. As I already told you, it was my day off yesterday. Miss Ottley only communicated with the upstairs maid, who helped her pack her suitcase. The maid informed me," Matthews said.

There was another silence while Carter waited for the butler to elaborate. He didn't.

Informed you of what! Carter screamed in his mind, but his voice remained steady. "Informed you of..."

"Miss Ottley told her she received a note from her mother, requesting she visit her in the south of France," Matthews reported.

For the second time in five minutes, Carter found himself at a loss for words.

"If there is nothing else, sir..." The butler stepped back as though to close the door.

It was obvious the gatekeeper was not going to be forthcoming with any useful information. Carter decided he needed to get inside to see if he could find some answers. "Yes, wait, there is something more."

"Sir?"

"When I was here the other night, I forgot my pen," Carter smiled apologetically. "I'd like to retrieve it. It was a gift from my late mother, you see, and it has great sentimental value to me. I'm sure you understand."

"Of course, sir. I'll fetch it for you," Matthews replied courteously. "Where did you leave it?"

"In the library, I believe, but no need to trouble yourself. I'll get it," Carter offered. "I know where it is. It will save time."

It took the butler a second or two to make up his mind. He swung the door open. "By all means, sir."

Carter smiled a thanks and stepped into the hall. "You needn't wait around for me. I'll let myself out, thank you."

Matthews gave a slight bow. "Very good, sir."

As the butler's footsteps echoed off into the distance, Carter went into the library. His eyes took in everything, not really knowing what he was expecting to discover or what to look for in the first place. He began a more close inspection of the room, and spotted a vacancy on one of the shelves. It struck him as strange since he remembered all the bookcases were full that night they worked on the message.

Then he recognized the vacant slot was where he had shelved Sharpe's *Egyptian Hieroglyphics*. The book had been removed.

Moving closer to investigate, he found another empty section on a lower shelf adjacent to the window. The spot was where he retrieved Champollion's *Dictionnaire égyptien en écriture hiéroglyphique*, *Précis du système hiéroglyphique des anciens Égyptiens*, and *Grammaire égyptienne*.

Those books were also missing.

He spun around to another set of shelves behind him.

All seven volumes of Brugsch's *Hieroglyphisch-demotisches Wörterbuch*: gone.

"Not exactly what I'd pack for a trip to the south of France for a reunion with a long-lost mother," Carter said to himself. *But something I'd need to translate a papyrus.*

He combed through the drawers and cabinets, growing more frustrated at his lack of uncovering anything that would provide a clue as to where May went. Halting in front of the fireplace, he swung open the painting and exposed the hidden safe. His fingers curled around the safe's handle, almost as an afterthought, and twisted. The knob refused to turn, the metal cold beneath his touch. What else would he expect?

He slumped against the mantle, wondering what his next move needed to be. He couldn't very well search the entire house on the pretense of trying to find a pen... but he should have one in case Matthews returned. Opening the table drawer, he pulled out a fountain pen.

He sighed and gazed into the fireplace grate, tapping the pen in one palm. The ashen remains of yesterday's fire still lay there, and he spotted a corner of paper protruding from underneath. Its surface was charred, but faint letters were visible.

Gingerly, he extracted the small scrap from the ashes. It contained portions of words, some crossed out, written in ink. He was positive it was May's handwriting. Matthews told him she had returned to the house the day previous. Maybe she had started a translation but something occurred... The door to the room opened and Carter dropped the scrap into the fireplace as Matthews entered the room.

"Were you able to find your pen, sir?" he asked.

"Yes, yes I did. Thank you." Carter held up the pen as evidence and slipped it into a pocket of the coveralls. He laughed in embarrassment. "It wasn't where I remembered putting it, though."

"Yes, sir." Matthews' response was noncommittal.

"Thank you, Matthews. Good day." Carter stepped out of the library and walked onto the stoop. The front door closed politely—but firmly—behind him.

He trudged back to his house, hands thrust deep into his pockets while his mind churned over the events of the day. Flicking through the post on the hall table when he arrived home, Carter paused at a single letter from his school. It was no doubt another cheerful reminder of the start of a new term.

Although he had no interest in its contents, he automatically carried the envelope into the parlor, where the housekeeper had kindly laid a fire in the grate before leaving for the day. Placing the envelope on the mantle and striking a match, Carter lit the kindling. As the flames licked around the logs, he sank into an armchair close by. His gaze traced aimless patterns in the dancing light as he thought.

His mind tried to untangle the facts and put them into some type of order. One: a note written by May lured him to the docks. There, his portion of the papyrus was stolen. Two: May had been successful in returning to her home. Based on what he found in the grate, she began translating her half of the papyrus. Three: she left the house for an unexpected trip to "the south of France," taking volumes from her library necessary for working on the translation.

Now all he needed was to fill in the missing bits... like why and where.

"Piece of cake," Carter mumbled to himself.

He shifted in the chair, the leather squeaking. Although he didn't want to think about it, the evidence pointed to one undeniable result: May had betrayed him. The idea weighed on him. He didn't want to believe that the note in her hand was an element of a nefarious plot. One he was not only a part of but an obstruction to... and so needed to be permanently removed.

She had started to translate the papyrus. That was clear. Yet without his half, her efforts would be fruitless. So she'd enlisted the assistance of those ruffians to steal his section of the papyrus... plus move him out of the picture at the same time. In case the thugs on the riverfront didn't compete their job, she created a story about the note from her mother. That way she could travel to an unknown location to complete her translation.

May told him that she would do anything to help her father. Did that include letting Carter's father die so the cure to their illness would be available only to Sir Robert? Did it involve Carter's murder? As he sorted through it, that line of thinking made too much sense, no matter what he wanted instead.

"No, no, no," Carter declared. He would not believe that May would do something like that. For once, he was going to push rationality aside for emotion.

The message she gave the upstairs maid about the purpose of her sudden travel plans keep running though his head... he couldn't help but think that was important. "A note from her mother in the south of France," he muttered to himself.

He recalled their conversation in the library that other night. May had told him she had no idea where her mother lived… "it could be in the south of France, for all I know," she had said.

Carter sat up in his seat as a thought struck him. May telling the upstairs maid that her mother had sent her a letter might have been a sign—a coded message—she hoped would reach Carter. After all, she could have come up with numerous reasons to leave the house—or just left without even giving one. Creating an excuse she and Carter knew was untrue may have been her way of communicating to him that she wasn't leaving by her own choice.

Which led to another conclusion: Dr. Belleville had coerced May into translating the ancient scroll, since he couldn't do it himself. Somebody had been dispatched to May's home to persuade her. Perhaps he threatened her with the likelihood of Sir Robert's impending death to force her to work on the translation. That would explain the missing books. May had to help him get his hands on Carter's piece of the papyrus, through a note written in her own handwriting.

But where did she go? The location Dr. Belleville could have secreted her was unknown. He slumped back into the chair with a groan. So his major problem remained: how to find her. Or the doctor, for that matter.

"Doctor! Of course, what's the matter with my brain!" Carter threw up his hands at his own stupidity. "He's a physician. The General Medical Council would have his details… even if they revoked his license, like Father said they did, they would still have an address. I'll look them up first thing in the morning. That's a beginning."

He had been sitting in front of the fireplace for longer than he thought, watching the orange and yellow flames flicker across the hearth. By now night had fallen. The room was dark and still, with only the faint crackling of burning logs to break the silence. Satisfied that he had at least the initial step for a plan of action, he rose to his feet and turned to leave, but stopped short with a start.

A shadowy figure outlined by the flickering firelight blocked the doorway. Determined not to be caught off guard like he was when he was attacked in the bathroom, Carter grabbed a fire poker, knocking over the other andirons with a loud clang in the process. He brandished his weapon.

Neither one moved as Carter squinted, trying to make out his mysterious visitor's face. Then, like clouds of the night sky peeling away to reveal the moon, the face's features slowly became revealed.

Large dark eyes stared out from beneath heavy brows. The face had a long, pointed chin with high cheekbones. Its nose was long and aquiline and its lips thin. Pointed ears lay flat along the sides of its skull.

It was the same face he had seen in the desert and outside the train window. But now Carter believed he had an idea who it was.

Carter lowered the poker. "Ptahmes?"

A flicker of recognition crossed the other's face, as though recognizing a dim memory from the distant past. He nodded—slight, barely noticeable.

"We know about the papyrus. We found it, but it was taken from us," Carter said in a rush, then growled at his own foolishness. Of course Ptahmes wouldn't understand Modern English. Even if Carter spoke in Arabic, they still couldn't communicate, since Arabic and the language of ancient Egypt were from two different families.

He glanced around the room, searching for a way to end this impasse. His gaze fell on the letter from his school resting on the mantle, and he got an idea. Dropping the poker, he reached into his pocket and pulled out the pen. He drew the two hieroglyph symbols for "I" and the three meaning "know" onto the back of the envelope with the dark, black ink.

Carter took slow, deliberate steps toward Ptahmes, as though approaching a strange dog, his written communication held between his two hands like an offering. He extended his arms and the envelope to the figure.

Ptahmes didn't reach out for it or make any other movements that acknowledged Carter's presence. Carter raised the paper up in front of the figure's face and angled it so the symbols would be illuminated by the firelight. Ptahmes' attention seemed to shift as his lifeless eyes stared intently at the hieroglyphs.

The fire in the grate began to flicker out and grow dim, as though under the control of an unseen entity. It finally went out, a thick blanket of darkness smothering the parlor. Carter tensed, not knowing what to expect, but he braced himself for an attack if it came, ready to fight back. Then just as fast as it had died down, the fire roared back with greater intensity.

The flames chased the shadows from the room, flooding the room in a sea of dancing red-orange light—but now, Carter was alone.

Carter arrived early in the morning at the General Medical Council building to start his search through their listings of registered physicians. After a few hours of paging through thousands of names, he found the entry he was looking for—Dr. William Belleville. He checked the record on why the doctor's license had been revoked. The physician had been prescribing unproven treatments, although what they were for and why they were given was not documented.

Regardless of all of that, Carter hoped that Dr. Belleville hadn't moved since the final notation in the register. Dr. Belleville was his first, and to be honest, his only, hope of finding May. Carter scrawled the last known address on a piece of paper and left the offices.

The air was crisp and cool, the sky a soft blue, and he reached his destination after a short walk. The street he stood on was a pleasant one, lined with pretty if not luxurious townhouses. Flowers, red ones blooming alongside some that were deep purple, adorned urns on the stoops of several dwellings. Carter strolled down the sidewalk, trying not to look too obvious as he searched for the number he wanted.

Carter came to a stop a few doors down from the address he'd written on the paper, careful to stay out of view of its windows. Now to determine if Dr. Belleville still was in residence. Then he saw something, and felt his hopes sink into the pit of his stomach. His quest may have ended before it had ever begun.

A "To Let" sign was secured to the wrought-iron fence outside the house, a removal van parked on the street, its back doors open. Two burly men emerged from the front door, struggling under the weight of a deep green sofa. They loaded it into the truck and made another trip inside.

Did that couch belong to Dr. Belleville or another family? Carter's plan was to follow Dr. Belleville and see if he led him to May. But how could he do that if he couldn't even keep up where he lived?

The address from the register was a few years old. Dr. Belleville may have moved in the intervening years, and somebody else could be occupying the building. Several "somebody elses" if he wanted to be truthful with himself. He needed to find who was moving house. Then he'd know whether to stick with his plan or try to come up with something new.

The answer presented itself. The two workmen left the house again and returned to their truck, one shutting the rear doors while the other climbed into the driver's seat. Following them out onto the stoop was Hassan Ali. The removal van drove off.

Carter pressed close to a bush so as not to be seen. So Dr. Belleville lived at that address—or did, until very a short time ago.

The question remained: Where was he moving to? And was May in the new location?

He cursed at not memorizing the company name on the van. He looked down the street to double-check the van, but it had already turned the corner. Using their records as an avenue of inquiry was now closed to him. He didn't have time to comb through all the removal firms in greater London.

Hassan Ali glanced around and stepped back inside, shutting the door. Carter decided to chance walking past the address, hoping he could discover some clue as to where Dr. Belleville had moved. As he strolled past, he cast a quick glance at the house. Through a ground floor window, he saw Hassan Ali pulling books off a shelf and packing them in a box. He turned to pick up something, and Carter quickly looked away. When he checked back, Hassan Ali was pasting a piece of paper to the carton he just filled. Carter continued his walk.

That might be a shipping tag, Carter thought, *with the new address on it. I need to get inside to take a peek at it...*

It only took him a dozen steps for the plan to form in his mind. But he'd require some outside help. And he knew just who to ask.

CHAPTER SEVENTEEN

"You look most presentable." Carter brushed off Kenton's coat, even though it didn't need it. The two of them stood in a small park around the corner from Dr. Belleville's house.

"I set this suit aside to wear upon the evening of my triumphant return to the theater," Kenton said with a touch of melancholy in his voice. The actor then brightened. "But it is nevertheless being employed for a noble cause... the one of unrequited love! Two star-crossed lovers!" He beamed at Carter.

Carter gave Kenton a weak smile, guilty for the lie he had told. He needed the old actor's help, but Carter couldn't very well let Kenton know the truth about May and Dr. Belleville. So instead he created an elaborate story about his "young lady's" father suddenly moving and forbidding Carter to see her anymore.

"You understand what you are to do," Carter said.

Kenton pulled himself up to his full height and assumed a wounded look. "Sir! I have trod the boards for over half my life!"

"Oh, yes, I know... I'm sorry... I didn't mean..." Carter mumbled in embarrassment.

"However, as we have no rehearsal time, we will review the scenario," Kenton declaimed. "I am to engage the servant on the pretense of desiring to let the property, and gain entry into the house. I will keep said servant occupied to permit you also to enter the premise surreptitiously, so you may search for a clue to the whereabouts of the location your young lady's dastardly father has secreted her."

He paused a second. "Reminds me of some of the melodramas I performed in the provinces whilst I learned my craft. The audiences in the hinterlands loved that kind of material."

"I don't know how much time it will take me once I get inside," Carter worried. "How long can you—"

Kenton cut him off with a flourish of one hand, as though wiping the thought out of mind. "Never fear, sir, never fear. I can fill whatever time is required. During one performance while essaying the role of Oberon in *Midsummer Night's Dream*, the actor playing the part of Puck became locked in the loo. I extemporized ten minutes of Shakespeare until the stage manager released him. The spectators never knew the difference."

He turned his attention to Carter. "Now, let us audition you, as you embark on your first foray into the noblest profession of them all."

Carter stepped back and stood as though a soldier being reviewed. Somewhere in the mass of clothing Kenton had in his house, he uncovered a uniform for a telegraph delivery boy. It almost fit Carter. Kenton looked the outfit up and down, one eyebrow cocked.

"It is fortunate you are only performing a walk-on part, so the ill-fitting costume is of no consequence." Kenton tapped his head. "Your cap, sir."

Carter put on the cap.

"No, no, sir! Not straight like that!" Kenton gestured. "Wear it at a rakish angle! You are playing the role of the gadabout messenger, devil-may-care, young and footloose!" Tilting the cap, Carter grinned. "Much better, much, much better! Adds to your character. Now, do you have your prop? An experienced actor always checks his props before the performance." Carter held up a blank telegram. "Excellent! Now, let's run over the cues."

"After I see you enter the house, I count to ten. Then I will walk down the block to the door, whistling *By the Light of the Silvery Moon*," Carter recited.

"Correct. When I perceive your song, I exeunt with the servant out of the hall, preferably upstairs," Kenton confirmed. He pointed at Carter to continue.

"I shall go inside and make my search," Carter went on. "As I leave, I am to sing *Let Me Call You Sweetheart*."

"Which will be my cue to exit stage right. Excellent!" Kenton concluded. "And now, Carter, the audience are settled in their seats, the orchestra has struck up the overture and the curtain is about to rise! Places! As we say in the theater, 'break a leg.'"

Carter grinned. "Break a leg."

Kenton closed his eyes, took a deep breath and opened them again. Pushing back his shoulders, he raised his chin and extended his arms outwards like he was about to begin a command performance for the Queen. He grabbed his silver-headed walking stick and walked away as if he owned the world. Carter watched him go with awe, understanding for the first time what Shakespeare meant when he said "All the world's a stage..." Indeed it was.

Carter couldn't resist the urge to peek around the corner and watch Kenton at work. The actor marched down the street, pausing only to throw a brief glance at the "To Let" sign near Dr. Belleville's front door before continuing up the steps to the entrance. After tapping the top of his cane against the wood, he waited for a response. When it didn't come fast enough, he rapped again. Hassan Ali opened the door.

Poor Hassan Ali never stood a chance. Carter chuckled as Kenton gestured animatedly to the "To Let" sign posted outside, then to the hallway beyond the door. Hassan Ali threw up his hands in an effort to deter Kenton's forwardness. He pointed emphatically back at the notice, but he might as well have tried to stand in the path of a steam locomotive to stop it. Kenton barreled through the door, brushing past Hassan Ali and swinging it shut with finality.

Carter counted to ten and commenced a jaunty walk down the sidewalk. As he neared the house he began whistling *By the Light of the Silvery Moon*. Stopping at the stairs leading to Dr. Belleville's residence, he glanced at the telegram, as if to verify he was at the correct address.

He silenced his tune, climbed up to the front door and pretended to ring the bell. After a few seconds, Carter leaned close to the entrance as if listening to somebody from within. He pushed open the door and stepped inside as though invited in. From upstairs, Kenton's voice echoed: "You call that a bathtub, sir? Why, it isn't big enough to wet a mouse!" Carter stifled a laugh and began his search.

The entry hall was devoid of any items, other than some hooks and a bit of wire hanging from the walls. Carter quickly checked the parlor, only to find it in the same state of emptiness. Stepping into the library, where he had seen Hassan Ali packing books, a glance revealed only empty shelves and no furniture. He muttered a curse under his breath. If he couldn't locate anything that could provide a lead on where Dr. Belleville and possibly May were, he would be lost.

He hastened toward the back of the house, walking through a vacant dining room. The kitchen was also completely bare, a few open cabinets emphasizing that fact as well as mocking his failure so far. Carter took off the cap and slapped it against his leg in frustration.

"The kitchen is down these stairs, I presume?" Kenton's voice boomed.

Carter glanced up at the back staircase, which led to the other floors, and saw a closed door next to it. Darting through, he found himself on the steps heading to the basement. He started down them and broke out in a grin when he reached the bottom.

The cellar contained stacks of wooden crates, some sealed and others still open. Shelves lined the walls, most empty but a few still cluttered with jars of liquids and vials of powders. It looked as if Dr. Belleville had been using the basement as a makeshift laboratory, which Hassan Ali was packing up for shipping. A blackened char mark marred the ceiling, as though a fire had recently taken place there.

A pile of labels and a pen rested on one crate. Hassan Ali must have been working on it when Kenton interrupted.

Carter glanced around before moving closer to the box. He had struck gold! An address was noted on the top label in bold, black handwriting: Dr. Wm. Belleville, Shadowplains House, Dartford. He grabbed the pen and scribbled down the address on a blank label, replacing the pen exactly in its original spot. With a satisfied smile, Carter tucked the paper away into his jacket.

Voices were coming from the kitchen, so he checked for another exit. A doorway in one wall would lead him out of the basement and put him at the bottom of the front steps. He clapped on his cap, slipped outside and moved upstairs to the street, taking a coin out of his pocket as he did so. With a grin on his face, like he had been given a generous tip, he chucked the coin in the air and caught it again.

"Let me call you 'Sweetheart,' I'm in love with you. Let me hear you whisper, that you love me too," Carter sang, albeit off-key. He strolled down the sidewalk, flipping the coin and continuing the song. "Keep the love-light glowing in your eyes so true. Let me call you 'Sweetheart,' I'm in love with you."

Carter arrived at the park and stopped. He took his find out his pocket and stared at the address he found, as though by doing so it would take him to his destination by magic. A few minutes later, Kenton joined him.

"Well, were you successful, Carter?" Kenton asked.

"Yes, sir!" Carter boasted, holding up the paper.

"Dartford?" Kenton mulled over as he read what was written on the paper, repeating the name under his breath. "I thought I had played every village and hamlet in Britain, but I do not recall that particular location."

"I'll check it in the atlas when I get home," Carter said, returning the label to his pocket. He bowed to Kenton. "Now, this walk-on, novice actor wearing the ill-fitting costume would like to take you to luncheon. In appreciation of your performance, if that is alright with you."

Kenton face lit up. "Of course, Carter, of course! It would be an honor! And we shall use the meal to plan the next act in your drama!"

Lush green fields, dotted with ancient oak trees and hedgerows that meandered along the narrow lanes surrounded the small village of Dartford. The landscape was gently undulating, creating a sense of serenity and isolation. In the distance, Carter caught glimpses of the meandering River Avon at the edge of the field.

The water glowed blue beneath a film of white mist hoisted high into the sky.

Carter stepped back to admire the tranquil vista in front of him, temporarily forgetting the reason for his journey. Yesterday's visit to the hospital made an unwanted return to his memory: the doctor's subtle but firm suggestion that Carter should make "final arrangements" for his father soon. Carter wanted to scream that he had another eight days left, at least that's what he thought by his figuring.

His frustration and grief bubbled up, threatening to surface, disabling him, but he pushed the emotions aside. He was here to find May and the papyrus—and together they would solve the mystery of his father and Sir Robert's illnesses.

Kenton suggested that Carter needed to disguise the true purpose of his visit to the small village, and even coached him as to his character. With that in mind, Carter assumed the persona of a botany student preparing for university.

His attire was appropriate for the role: tweed trousers and coat, a white shirt, brown boots, plus a matching hat. A canvas knapsack slung over his back and a tall walking staff in one hand completed his costume. Kenton also insisted that Carter wear a pair of wire-rimmed spectacles, which he had provided. Although the prescription wasn't strong, everything still became blurry when Carter put them on, so he left them in his pocket. Dartford didn't have a railroad station, so Carter got off the train at a nearby town and embarked on the eight-mile walk to the tiny village.

It consisted of a cluster of quaint buildings, their stonework aged by time. Each cottage was distinct, with bright flower boxes accenting the window ledges. Wisteria and roses clung to the walls, creating a peaceful tapestry. A well-kept green anchored the center of the village. An ancient oak tree stood guard in the middle, its bent branches reaching for the sky. Wooden benches were scattered around the quiet spot.

Carter sat at one of the outside tables at the local pub, The Thistle & Hare, its inviting thatched roof and timber-framed exterior across the lane from the green. He pulled a copy of *Wayside and Woodlands Blooms* from his knapsack and slipped on the glasses. In a moment, the landlord came up to the table.

"Afternoon, sir," the man said, wiping his hands on his apron. "What do you fancy?"

"Oh, good afternoon." Carter spoke in a somewhat higher-pitched voice than usual—another Kenton touch—and removed his spectacles. "I'd like the ploughman's lunch, please."

"An excellent choice, sir. We do a very good one, we do." The landlord gestured to the staff. "Just passing through, are you?"

"Oh, yes. I'm a botany student, and I'm on a walking tour of the area." Carter smiled as he tapped the book on the table. "I want to take in the local flora before university begins."

The man glanced down at the open pages. "Flowers, eh? Then perhaps you help out the wife." He pointed to a clump of blue blooms growing next to the pub. "What is the name of those? The missus would like to know."

Carter looked at the plant. "Oh, those? Why... why, that's a zahra jameela haqan." He hoped he made the Arabic translation of "really pretty flower" sound at least close to Latin.

The landlord looked puzzled. "So that's a zahra..."

"Zahra jameela haqan," Carter said again slowly.

The man repeated the name. "Right. Thanks. I'll fetch your lunch."

The landlord headed back inside the pub but soon returned. He set down a plate featuring a selection of cheeses, pickles, crusty bread and cold meats in front of Carter.

"Thank you. It looks delicious," Carter said while he paid. "Oh, before you go, have you heard of Shadowplains House? It's supposed to be located around here."

"It's about four miles down the road." The man tilted his head in the direction as he took Carter's coins. "What do you want with that place?"

"My friend told me of a spectacular display of Hyacinthoides non-scripta on the grounds," Carter enthused, glad he remembered the caption of the last picture on the page he had looked at.

"Well, you've got a good day for it." The man gave the polite grin of somebody who wasn't quite sure of what Carter was talking about, then went back inside the pub.

Carter had no idea how famished his hike had left him until he began to wolf down his lunch, devouring it all. With his plate empty, he tucked away his book and hoisted his knapsack onto his shoulders. He picked up his walking staff and headed out on the road toward Dr. Belleville's new estate.

He was familiar with the sight of country houses. They were usually built from native stone or bricks, boasting an ostentatious facade decorated with a mix of architectural styles, from Tudor and Jacobean to Georgian and Victorian. The driveway would be long and bordered by old yews, leading to the grand entrance, which often boasted a porte cochère—a sheltered porch for carriages. Perfectly manicured gardens and terraced lawns would ring the house like quilt pieces, ancient trees standing watch all around it—all this would make up the property. A serene lake might even grace the property.

Shadowplains House was nothing like that—instead it exuded the air of a prison, looming large and hostile over the landscape. It was an ungainly monstrosity, constructed from gray stone and jutting from the earth with no sense of aesthetics or beauty in whatever design it had. Its windows, like blind eyes, stared across the grounds of wild grasses and half-dead trees that lined the drive up to the entrance.

Carter put on the glasses, pulling his hat down until the brim almost rested upon his nose. He darted a glance at the house as he strolled past. The curtains were drawn, and he thought he heard the distant sound of a radio. He knew there was only one way to discover if Dr. Belleville—and May—were in there. It was time to go for a looksee.

When he reached a cluster of trees next to the road just past the house, he stopped, pulling off the glasses. He hid his walking staff, knapsack and hat in a thicket of brush before peering through the foliage at the building.

His choices were limited: it would be too bold to march up to the front door. Throwing pebbles at the windows, like something from a cheap penny dreadful, wouldn't work either. That left him to attempt sneaking in through a back or side door.

Carter scanned the area. Some ragged bushes and remains of a hedgerow stood between him and the house. He crept out of the protective cover of the trees and kept low to the ground, skirting around the foliage until he had reached the side of the house. Pressing his back against the rough stone wall, he worked himself down to the corner of the building, ducking under windows. He peeked around the edge. A door was visible.

Creeping up to it, he grasped the doorknob. As he slowly twisted, his grip tightened in anticipation. He felt a cold click. The door was locked.

Carter let out an annoyed sigh, then spotted an old window just above a drainpipe on the ground. He suspected that it led to the basement, so he bent down to peer through the grime-covered glass. All he could make out in the blackness was a void beyond the glass.

Hooking his fingers into the frame, he lifted. Cautiously, he peered inside for any sign of life, but all remained quiet. Taking a deep breath, he summoned one last effort and with a sudden jerk managed to wrench open a narrow gap—just wide enough for him to squeeze through—before anyone could potentially spot him. He wriggled inside and, with only a whisper of sound, dropped into the basement below.

He was in part of the basement, a small room illuminated only by stray beams of light that shone through the single window he just used to enter. The air was damp and musty, and dirt coated the stone floor beneath his feet. A radio played somewhere in the house—it sounded like a Bach concerto—adding an eerie quality to the shadows of the room. Boxes and crates, most likely the contents of Dr. Belleville's laboratory from the London house, filled the area.

There were two closed doors on opposite sides of the room. Carter weighed his options, then walked towards the one on his right. Sliding the bolt to one side, its metal latch released. He pulled it open and stepped through, the door clicking shut by itself behind him.

He was in another storage room, windowless and dark. Carter turned to leave, then stood still for a moment as he realized something was off. His breath caught in his throat when he felt the presence of another in the pitch-black storeroom. It overwhelmed him with the same terror as when he was attacked in the bathtub. He reached for the door.

Long, bony fingers tightened on his neck from behind, crushing him with an iron grip. He struggled against it, but nothing but air passed through his desperate, flailing, grasp. With a surge of strength, he took hold of the skeletal hands strangling him.

Roaring with fury, he ripped apart the deathly grasp and spun around, grabbing the attacker by its middle. He flung it up with all his might before violently slamming it back down to the ground.

Carter scrambled out the door, shutting it behind him and sliding the bolt closed. He leaned against the boards, panting, then realized he was holding onto something. Looking down, he gave a cry when saw what it was.

He held a tight-clenched human hand.

CHAPTER EIGHTEEN

The hand appeared as though it came from a mummy. It was snapped from the forearm, near the wrist, and was jagged at the edges. The bone had broken like glass. But it was a unique mummy's hand. The flesh was leathery and pliable, not stiff or brittle.

Carter pulled at its fingers, and they sprung back to their original position when he released him. The skin was a very dark brown, exquisitely preserved. Even the veins and arteries were still visible, looking like strands of black thread.

"Ptahmes," Carter whispered to himself, thinking of what was on the other side. Dr. Belleville had succeeded... he had revived the ancient priest from the tomb. The hand must have come off during the struggle.

"You've met our house guest, I suppose."

Carter whirled around. He had been so intent on the risen mummy that he didn't hear Dr. Belleville and Hassan Ali enter the basement by the other door. Hassan Ali aimed a revolver directly at Carter's head.

Dr. Belleville grinned, then saw what Carter held. "Oh dear, oh dear. Did that come from him?" He gestured toward the bolted door and clucked his tongue. "Our boarder hasn't been here too terribly long and is not at all content about the situation. This accident will only add to his ill-humor."

Carter found his voice. "How long... how long has he been..."

"Risen from the dead? Not much time, perhaps twelve hours or so," Dr. Belleville said. "Surprisingly, for a priest who predicted and arranged for his own resurrection, he seems to be rather put out about it, in fact. It took both of us to lock him in there, but Hassan Ali offered to explain the situation to him. With the assistance of a whip, if necessary."

The shock started to wear off for Carter. His brain began to function normally again. "May... Miss Ottley..."

"Miss Ottley's translation of the final papyrus—the one you so rudely ripped in two—provided the method to revive Ptahmes," Dr. Belleville said. "When Hassan Ali visited Miss Ottley at her home, she refused to give up her part of the papyrus or translate it. He informed her that I had captured you, at the time a falsehood. When he produced your half of the papyrus as proof, her attitude changed.

"Hassan Ali added that 'she didn't know what a pleasure I was having planning to torture you', and I was going 'to make you suffer like the damned' if she didn't comply with my demands. Perhaps gilding the lily, but it worked. She became most cooperative when she thought you were going to be harmed. You should be a happy young man. She appears to be quite taken with you. Her feelings for you were such that she finished her task in a single day, without any rest."

"Where is she now?" Carter demanded.

"Upstairs, in an exhausted, and, if I might add, drugged, sleep." Dr. Belleville nodded at the door. "Ptahmes was—or is, I don't know what verb tense to use—a genius, but his process for reanimating is cumbersome. That's not unexpected given the science of his time. This is where my considerable intellect comes into play. I believe I know what modifications the procedure requires to make it more efficient and meet my requirements more completely."

"What are these requirements of yours?" Carter asked.

"I will tell you in time. Now, as for you, I have a special role... my new test subject." Dr. Belleville extracted a slim, mahogany box from his coat pocket. He opened it and held up a syringe, full of a black sludge that resembled used oil.

"Similar to my father and Sir Robert?" Carter retorted.

"They served quite well, and those experiments succeeded, but I need to trial my revised formula. I am also quite near to an improved reviving serum." Dr. Belleville gave a slight press to the plunger of the hypodermic, triggering a fine spray of mist from the needle. "Kindly remove your jacket and roll up one shirt sleeve."

"And if I refuse? Will you take pleasure in torturing me into compliance, as you threatened to May?" Carter fired back.

"Mr. Pinsent, I am not only a surgeon, I am a skillful surgeon. I am, besides, a vivisectionist. It is one of my hobbies. I can keep you alive and conscious quite a long time during a live dissection. Hours, in fact. As much as I would enjoy the procedure, given your insolence and interference, the effects would irreparably damage you as a useful specimen." Dr. Belleville flashed a sardonic smile. "No, today I present clearer options: a temporary living death, or the real thing."

Hassan Ali cocked the revolver and moved around, placing the gun's barrel against Carter's temple.

"That is providing me with a rather Hobson's choice, is it not?" Carter asked.

Dr. Belleville gave a disinterested shrug.

Carter sighed and took off his jacket, dropping it to the floor. He rolled up the left sleeve of his shirt.

"I knew you would respond to reason." Dr. Belleville grinned. He jabbed the syringe into Carter's arm.

Carter winced as the hypodermic pierced his skin, injecting the searing serum into his vein. Instantly, his arm burned like it was being consumed by fire, spreading through his body, his bloodstream becoming a raging inferno. He grimaced as the intense heat climbed to his shoulder, scorching each nerve in its path before engulfing his chest. His torso became a blazing furnace.

As the formulation reached his lungs, they seemed to crumple and harden like dried leather, and his heart slowed, an eternity between each beat. With every passing second, more of his muscles and tissues succumbed to the burning pain. At last, his legs gave out and he collapsed on the ground.

The fire suddenly was extinguished, replaced with numbing cold. He fought to prevent the serum from penetrating his brain, to remain conscious, but he failed. Nerve fibers ignited with an intense, blinding light. His vision blurred and narrowed until it was like he was trapped in a suffocating tunnel that closed in on him.

Then he knew no more.

Carter floated in the air, looking down at his own body on the examination table like a bystander. His clothes were gone, and he wore a linen cloth wrapped around his waist like a diaper. Dr. Belleville stood on one side, studying Carter's still form while holding a hypodermic in one hand. On the other loomed Hassan Ali, scribbling notes in a leatherbound notebook. Dr. Belleville pulled the needle out of Carter's arm and spoke to Hassan Ali in hushed tones, but Carter couldn't make out their words.

Dr. Belleville set the syringe down on a metal tray before taking hold of Carter's wrist to check his pulse. He gave a nod and said something to Hassan Ali, which he wrote down in the notebook. Gently he lifted Carter's eyelids with his fingers and examined his eyes.

Violent convulsions wracked the body laying below him. Carter snapped back to his physical form, his eyes opening in shock and confusion. The seizure was over quickly, but left him weak and disoriented, as if he had just been ripped from a deep slumber.

Dr. Belleville and Hassan Ali helped him off the examination table and to an iron chair bolted to the floor. Carter tried to resist, but his limbs refused to respond to his brain.

They forced him into the unforgiving seat. Dr. Belleville secured metal rings around his wrists, trapping him in place along the chair arms, while another ring enclosed his chest, pressing him against the unyielding back of the chair.

Dr. Belleville picked up a small vial that sat next to the tray, then took the notebook from Hassan Ali. He placed them inside a doctor's bag and carried it to a glass cabinet, placing it on the top shelf. With one parting glance at Carter, he and Hassan Ali left the room.

Carter put his head back, his mind shrouded in a dense fog. He shut his eyes and started taking breaths to help his brain clear. With a final deep inhale, he opened his eyes and took in his surroundings.

The room was devoid of any windows, illuminated only by the electric lights hanging from the ceiling. The door was an imposing structure, upholstered with layers of cushioned leather to muffle any sound that may escape. The floor was covered in thick rubber, most likely providing a strange springiness underfoot.

As his senses cleared, Carter realized that this place was no ordinary room. It was a chemical laboratory. At least half a dozen tables were scattered about, cluttered with retorts, dynamos and various testing tubes and instruments. Glass cases lined the walls, displaying porcelain boxes and delicate vials of drugs, while large jars filled with bubbling acids sat on shelves above them.

But what caught Carter's eye was the casket-sized enclosure made entirely of glass panels resting on top of a metal box base.

It was raised about three feet off the ground on two sturdy steel trestles.

The sound of a broom scraping the floor came from behind Carter. As much as he strained, he could not turn his head far enough to see who was in the room. He called out, "Hello? Who's there?"

The sweeping ceased, and footsteps approached the chair. They shuffled past and stopped in front of Carter.

Ptahmes stood in front of him, his blood-red eyes fixed on Carter with a glazed, emotionless stare. He wore a long, shapeless yellow robe and leather sandals on his feet. One hand held a broom, and very slowly he extended his other arm before Carter's face. He gasped with shock that the hand was gone. It had been severed from the wrist and nothing but a stump remained.

Carter glanced over at the table where Dr. Belleville had tossed the mummified hand Carter had clutched after his struggle in the basement storeroom. It was Ptahmes' missing hand. But—but—of course a hand thousands of years old perhaps, one that could not have grown upon a man who was alive and breathing.

Alive! Breathing!

Carter gazed in awe at the figure that stood before him, a living mummy. He had only encountered Ptahmes as a ghostly form previously, so seeing him in flesh and blood was a remarkable experience. But then again, could he be considered "flesh and blood"? Or for that matter, "alive"?

In many ways, he appeared like the other mummies Carter had seen. The skin was of exactly the same color as the detached hand. It had the same brown, shriveled appearance, the same leather-like texture.

Carter leaned as far forward as the restraints would allow as he saw that, unless he was dreaming, Ptahmes did not appear to breathe. His nostrils were fallen in and glued together. How then did he breathe? Not a movement of his body disclosed the smallest sign of respiration.

Carter couldn't tear his gaze away from Ptahmes, a mixture of horror and fascination consuming him. Ptahmes' features were frozen in a rigid expression, with his mouth sealed shut. Yet, there was an eerie sense of life in the gaunt body in front of him—some controlling force behind the animated corpse. As if on cue, his handless arm fell to his side as he continued to stare unblinkingly at Carter.

Upon closer examination, the lidless eyes seemed to reflect light rather than produce it. The cornea was only a thin, gelatinous layer filled with wrinkles that refracted light from all angles. His dead-looking eyes lacked pupils, the irises appearing as dull red balls. The whites were covered by opaque black film, giving no indication of life within.

The two looked at each other, a mere few feet apart but separated by thousands of years. Carter stared at the ancient Egyptian priest. He wondered if any glimmer of recognition registered that Carter was the same one Ptahmes had visited before.

After a few moments, Ptahmes moved to a nearby table and bent over it. He appeared to be writing, but Carter was not sure. He heard a curious, raucous scratching sound. Carter closed his eyes and surrendered to the unbelievable truth unfolding in front of him. Perhaps ten minutes passed when the noises stopped. With a jolt, Carter's eyes popped open, and he was met with Ptahmes' stern gaze.

The ancient priest held in his hand a slate covered in hieroglyphs. As grateful as Carter was for his years of studying the language, he couldn't help but curse his own imperfections and lapses in memory. He could decipher most of the message, but there were still pieces that eluded him.

"It is not meet that Ptahmes—named Tahutimes—son of Mery, son of Hap, High Priest of Amen-Ra and the Hawk-headed Horus, should be a wicked unbeliever's slave..." Carter read. "Death explains... The spirit of a good man hurried hence accuses me unanswered at the ... throne... For time unending... Fanet... King of all the Gods..."

The writing ended at the bottom of the slate. Carter looked at Ptahmes and nodded. The living cadaver shuffled back to the table, wiped off the chalk and wrote again. After perhaps another ten minutes, Ptahmes returned, extending the tablet toward Carter again.

"Thus only shall you escape the death that threatens," Carter continued to read. "You shall swear to break my stele of ivory, to commit my papyri to the flames unread, to burn my body and scatter my ashes to the winds of Heaven. You shall swear by

Amen-Ra, King of Earth and Heaven, to destroy... the oppressor and our enemy."

Again, the writing had run out of space. Carter nodded once more, and Ptahmes made a trip back to the table. Another ten minutes or so passed as he scratched more hieroglyphs onto the slate.

Burn my body and scatter my ashes to the winds of Heaven. That sentence startled Carter. Cremation was not a common practice among the ancient Egyptians. Their burial customs revolved around preserving the body to ensure an afterlife for the deceased. It was believed that without a body, the Ka and Ba would have no existence in the world beyond, erasing that person's identity.

Ptahmes' grand plan for his resurrection was an almost-complete failure. While he may have returned to life, or some version of living, it was not in the way he had intended. He ended up not as an elite member of society as he once was, but as an unwilling servant of somebody like Dr. Belleville. It was understandable that Ptahmes now longed for the peace of nothingness. Carter was sorry for the old priest.

Ptahmes came back to Carter and held out the slate one more time. "He has deciphered the inscriptions. He has mastered their meaning. He knows. He cannot be permitted to live lest I... and he the enemy exalt himself and triumph over you and me... Swear then, and aid shall be accorded in your hour of need."

Such was the deal Ptahmes offered to Carter: if he agreed to kill Dr. Belleville and destroy the papyri and an ivory stele that the doctor possessed, Ptahmes would assist Carter. However, there was one condition—Carter must not attempt to read the documents; the secrets must die with the priest. In addition, he was to burn the mummified body in order to put Ptahmes' troubled spirit to rest.

The wildness and unreality of situation didn't register for Carter. The proposal before him was both grave and serious, and he treated it as such. If he accepted, he would be obliged to follow through with the assistance promised. Destroying the stele and papyri, and even burning Ptahmes' mummy, those he'd perform ... but killing Dr. Belleville? Could he justify taking such drastic measures? Belleville deserved punishment for his actions, but did Carter have the right to swear on his life to terminate another's? As much as he despised Dr. Belleville, could he actually carry out the task? Could he kill another human being?

Carter certainly wasn't in a position to negotiate. In the end, he decided that at least turning Dr. Belleville over to the police would fulfill his part of the bargain. The doctor had committed enough crimes to guarantee a trip to the gallows. Carter wouldn't have to commit the killing. The crown would take care of that.

He looked up into the dead, blood-red eyes of the ancient Egyptian priest. He spoke in the most solemn tone he was able to muster.

"Ptahmes, son of Mery, son of Hap, once High Priest of Amen-Ra, but now I know not what—I swear by the King of Earth and Heaven to destroy the stele and papyri unread if I shall find them, to burn your body and scatter the ashes and to kill your enemy and mine." He repeated what he said in Arabic.

After a pause, the dark, fixed, corpse-like face of Ptahmes turned away from Carter. He pressed the slate to his chest with the stump of his left wrist and with the right hand rubbed out the hieroglyphic writing. He then glided over to the table and replaced the tablet.

Carter's eyes tracked every move Ptahmes made, anticipating his release from the chair. But instead of returning, the living mummy shuffled out of view, leaving Carter alone and still bound. He waited several minutes, but the Ptahmes didn't return. Why hadn't Ptahmes set him free as promised? Did he understand Carter agreed to his conditions?

In desperation, Carter fought against the straps like a monkey rattling his cage at the zoo, the clanging of metal echoing in the space. "Ptahmes! Where are you?" he yelled, his voice filled with fear and confusion.

The only response was the sound of the broom sweeping across the floor.

CHAPTER NINETEEN

Sometime later, the door behind Carter opened and closed. Dr. Belleville walked in, pistol in hand. He checked Carter's pulse, then pulled a chair in front of him and sat.

"Are you cool? What I mean is, are you perfectly collected? Do you feel able to engage in conversation? Or are you too dazed—or perhaps too angry?" Dr. Belleville asked, doctor to patient.

"I can promise at least to listen and try to understand you," Carter returned.

"The underdog is a fool to be sarcastic," Dr. Belleville said dryly.

"Why the weapon?" Carter extended an index finger at the revolver. "I am as helpless as a trussed fowl."

"You've managed to escape from other situations before," Dr. Belleville said.

"The coffin?"

The doctor smiled. "That. Besides, we are not the only ones in this room."

"Ptahmes?" Carter nodded toward the sound of the sweeping. "Are you afraid of him?"

"I fear nothing living, young man," Dr. Belleville said with contempt.

Anything living, Carter thought. An idea came into his head. Maybe he could use Dr. Belleville's belief in the unseen world against him.

"You may think you have me laid here quite nicely by the heels, Dr. Belleville." Carter's tone became threatening. "But you're not the only one who has a knowledge of the old magic arts of ancient Egypt. I've visited there for years, and studied the old ways for just as long, longer than you. I tell you to your face that I possess a charm no less powerful than the one you found in the tomb. And if you force me to, I will use it."

Dr. Belleville stood up at once, surprised, incredulous but also a little troubled and dubious, it seemed to Carter. "You think you can bluff me?" he snarled.

But Carter had bluffed him. He could read it in his eyes. Carter answered him with nothing but a smile.

The doctor assumed a sneer, his eyes glinting. He picked up the revolver, cocked the gun and put it to Carter's temple. "Well, you've challenged me," he jeered. "In just one minute I'll blow your brains out. The effectiveness of your 'charm' is now in question!"

Carter realized his thought about Dr. Belleville was on target... too much on target. His nerves had been shaken by what Carter had said, and he intended to kill Carter in order to restore his own sense of security. And nothing could prevent him.

Dr. Belleville started to count aloud. "One, two, three, four..."

Desperation seized Carter, providing the courage to continue. He recalled Neitenstein at the seance and began to perform in a similar manner. "Look in my eyes," he shrieked at him. "And listen if you want to live. Listen if you dare."

Dr. Belleville looked at Carter. Carter put all the strength of his existence into his gaze, and a strange, wild thrill of exultation ran through him as he saw Dr. Belleville's eyes dilate after encountering the glance thrown at him.

"My death means yours," Carter hissed. "My monitor stands over you. You'll be shriveled as by lightning. We'll go together before the throne of God and accept His judgment! Maybe He will have mercy on you, but I doubt it. Now shoot if you will and your soul will be damned for all eternity! Shoot—go on, get it over with. Shoot!"

But Dr. Belleville did not fire. His hand fell to his side. He staggered back, staring at Carter open-mouthed until the chair stopped him. Carter spotted his advantage and pressed it home.

"Stop!" Carter shouted. "If you value your dirty little life, halt! Stand still and do not turn your head. One movement and we both die."

Dr. Belleville stood like a frozen image. Locking eyes, Carter began to mutter in a sing-song way a string of meaningless Egyptian phrases. To more powerfully impress the superstitious fool, all of a sudden Carter uttered a loud heart-rending groan and slumped forward against the metal band encircling his chest.

"I give you my compliments," Dr. Belleville said in cold, slow, even tones after a pause. He put the revolver down. "You have a quick wit and a nerve of iron. I admire you for that, but I need you alive. You are my subject, and we have tests to complete..." He bared his teeth just as Carter had seen a jackal grin. "So many, many tests."

"I've bound your fate with mine by ties no mortal can break." Carter tried to continue the ruse. "You cannot scare me, because you cannot harm me without hurting yourself—and in your depths of heart, you know it."

"Enough of that rubbish," Dr. Belleville retorted harshly. "You can't fool me twice. Scream all you want. This room is soundproof. The previous owner of this house used it as an indoor shooting range."

"You'll see when the time comes—if you have the courage," Carter said in a veiled voice. "You'll die when I die!

Dr. Belleville burst out laughing, but there was a note of nervousness in his mocking mirth that pleased Carter. "Bah!" he said at last. "Would you sit there trussed up like a chookie skewered for the table if you had the power you pretend?"

He returned to the chair and sat. He began to pluck at his beard. "I came in here to ask you how you're feeling, but in your present mood I doubt if your answer would be truthful or even civil. Fortunately, simple observation will provide much of the information I require. Your pulse rate is about half what I would expect from somebody in your particular situation. Your respiration also presents as remarkably slow, given the same reason."

His eyes swept up and down Carter's body. "Your muscular vigor appears excellent. In fact, your muscles may have actually increased in size somewhat." He closed his eyes and let out a breath in anger. He shouted, "Stop sweeping!"

The rasp of the broom against the floor went on.

Dr. Belleville's face twisted into a snarl as he stormed past Carter, out of his sight and to the back of the room. The sound of a wooden broom handle hitting the ground echoed, followed by muffled grunts and shuffling feet. Finally, with an irritated voice, Dr. Belleville commanded: "Sit! Sit down there! Sit! Sit!"

More scrabbling on the floor, and Dr. Belleville returned to Carter's side. The door opened again. Hassan Ali entered the room, carrying a tray set with cold meats and water which he placed on a little table and wheeled before Carter.

"I'm not proposing to starve you to death," Dr. Belleville said, making a sweeping gesture over the food. "You've been—let's see—at least sixty hours without eating."

"Sixty!" Carter gasped. "Impossible."

"It's a fact. You have been unresponsive for two and a half days," Dr. Belleville said as he picked up the gun.

He unsnapped the clamp holding Carter's right hand with his free hand. He stood over Carter with a revolver while Carter ate, watching for a few minutes with a sort of part-contemptuous, part-amused curiosity. "Here's another observation. You are not clearing the board in the fashion of a famished wolf. Either you have extraordinary self-control or you're not that hungry."

"I'm not that hungry," Carter responded, surprised.

"Interesting," Dr. Belleville said. "Your decreased appetite, heart rate and respiration all indicate that the effects from the condition of suspended animation I placed you in has impacted your physiology, even after your revival." Carter kept eating, while Dr. Belleville silently observed him with a peculiar fascination, as if watching a strange and intricate mechanical man.

The sixty-hour time lag initially worried Carter. It cut into the literal deadline for his father and Sir Robert by almost three days. But then another idea crossed his mind. His lack of hunger may be evidence that his slower metabolism meant his body required less sustenance to stay alive. If that were true, the same could be the case for his father and Sir Robert. Perhaps they had more time than he and May originally thought.

After Carter finished eating, Hassan Ali bound Carter's arm to the chair again, standing behind him to do it. He picked up the tray, flashing the mocking grin of the prisoner becoming the warden, and left the room. Carter and Dr. Belleville gazed at each other in silence for a moment.

"I was planning to test your intelligence and communication skills, to determine their status after a period of suspended animation," Dr. Belleville said, "but based on your attempt to bluff me, I don't think that is necessary. Just as it was unnecessary in the other case." He gave a disgusted wave toward the mummy.

Carter twisted in his seat as much as the bonds would permit, catching a glimpse of Ptahmes seated on a chair, hands on his knees. He returned his gaze to Dr. Belleville.

"He is a nothing more than a zuvembie," Dr. Belleville dismissed.

"A what?"

"An animated corpse," Dr. Belleville explained. "A zuvembie is not human anymore. It cannot talk or think like a living person. The term is from the West Indies. There, some of the dead are raised through witchcraft to become slaves to work on the sugar cane plantations."

"There's no thought? No language? So Ptahmes can't communicate to you, or you to him?"

Dr. Belleville shook his head. "No thought. Only very primitive communication."

Carter suppressed a smile. He wasn't the only one trying to bluff Dr. Belleville. Ptahmes was doing so as well, and succeeding.

"Ptahmes was certainly clever, indeed a genius, but he made some fatal mistakes." Dr. Belleville chuckled to himself a moment to revel in his own wit. He pulled out a silver flask and filled a small cup, sipping it slowly. He leaned towards Carter, clearly believing that he was much smarter and wanting to make sure Carter was aware of it.

"Firstly, the oil was only applied after he died, and secondly, he never ingested it internally." He drained his drink. "So what happened? While his external body was preserved, the internal tissues were damaged by death. It seems that his brain stem and cerebellum are mostly intact, allowing for some motor and vegetative functions. However, his higher cognitive skills such as language and logical thought have been wiped clean."

The doctor looked at the mummy with scorn. "In some ways, he is like an infant... he loves playing with the light switch, for example. He also can be taught to perform basic tasks, but he has to be trained like a dog."

"But that has not happened to me," Carter said.

Dr. Belleville said, "For that, you can thank *my* genius. I analyzed the oil from the tomb, and created a liquid form I could use as an injection. After I experimented on stray animals, I was ready to move on to larger mammals."

Rage welled up in Carter at Dr. Belleville's condescending reference to his father and Sir Robert. He almost made an angry retort but stopped at the last moment. He tried to make his voice sound as neutral as possible. "Oh? And one was Sir Robert?"

"Yes. Sir Robert threatened my plans," Dr. Belleville said as he poured himself another drink. "He only thought of the mummy in terms of advancement for his career as an eminent Egyptologist. The fool."

Carter had to understand Dr. Belleville's goals before figuring out his next move. He decided to play on his ego. "That's very smart. Remove an obstacle and obtain a test subject at the same time."

"Upon my soul, I enjoy a chat with you. You are a bright lad," Dr. Belleville said to Carter as he took another sip. "You see, I have no one else to confide in..." —he waved toward Ptahmes—"...who's intelligent. Besides, there's an odd pleasure in speaking to a helpless enemy."

Gloating, you mean, Carter thought. "I understand your logic behind Sir Robert, but what about my father?"

"The mummy's existence was to be kept secret," Dr. Belleville said, "but the robbery at the tomb brought you and your father into the picture. That complicated affairs."

"So you used my father as the second subject while I was away on my... ocean voyage, shall we say?" Carter asked. "You did arrange for that, didn't you?"

Dr. Belleville chuckled. "Of course I did! But you weren't supposed to return. My agents in Port Said did not carry out my orders properly."

"I guess I should be thankful for their incompetence. And where does Miss Ottley fit in?"

"I needed her for her skills in translation. She was never in any danger," Dr. Belleville said.

Carter nodded in appreciation. "I must say, you had everything very well planned, well executed. Quite intelligently done."

Dr. Belleville beamed. He raised the cup in a toast.

"But I'm still not sure why you are interested in Ptahmes' preservation method," Carter said. "To gain immortality?"

"Bah! Immortality is impossible," Dr. Belleville gave a dismissive laugh. "No, sir, not for immortality, but for an extended life span. That has always been my quest, the scope of my practice."

"Is that why you lost your license?"

"Those idiots at the General Medical Council and their feeble, small minds!" Dr. Belleville spat out. "Why should man be allotted such a short, miserable season here on Earth? Answer me that. It is a waste of precious time, a cruel joke. What can be accomplished in a mere seventy years or so? What goals cannot be completed?" He gave a wolf-like grin. "What pleasures are never experienced?"

He leaned toward Carter, eyes bright. "Now consider a lifespan of one hundred, five hundred, or even a thousand years! Now imagine what people will pay for that opportunity!" He sat back, a broad smirk of success on his face. "Millions, sir, millions!"

Carter was quiet while he thought before he spoke. "You injected me. Do I have a prolonged life now?"

"That is not clear as of yet," Dr. Belleville said. "Ptahmes' formula, when used as a serum, causes suspended animation, but the person is unconscious. That is not the most attractive way to spend an extended lifetime. My refinement returns the subject to a conscious state, but apparently with a much slower metabolism. That should reduce stress on the internal organs, less wear and tear on the machine, so to speak, allowing it to last longer.

You are currently exhibiting that, at least at a cursory glance. I have to examine you completely, observe you over time and complete some tests to determine if your physiology has been affected in a permanent or temporary manner. Additional treatments might be required, as well as adjustment of doses. This, of course, will take time." Dr. Belleville poured himself another drink.

"So I never leave here." Carter's voice was soft.

"I'm afraid I can't permit my subject to be running around loose. I must control for all possible variables. The injection doesn't grant immunity to disease, or protection from accidents. It wouldn't do to have you hit by an omnibus now, would it?"

Dr. Belleville said. "I don't want my work smeared over a London street."

"And what of Miss… what happens to May?"

"Obviously, she must remain too, as she knows too much. She too will not leave." Dr. Belleville leered at Carter. "Come, come, you should be pleased with that. After all, man was not meant to live alone. You two will be reunited, and I will allow nature to take its course." He held both hands up in the air. "Your offspring will be remarkable! I wonder how their genetics will be affected."

"You plan to breed us like cattle!" Carter couldn't control himself further and spat at Dr. Belleville. He laughed.

"More on the arrangements for you and Miss Ottley later. At present, there is one more treatment to be given."

"What do you mean?"

Dr. Belleville gestured toward Ptahmes. "When you first saw the mummy, you commented on how well preserved it was."

Carter nodded.

Dr. Belleville gestured towards Carter, taking in his entire body. "You are now a handsome, well-built youth. My serum preserves the internal functions, but not the body's external appearance. You will be young and fit on the inside, but your true age would still be visible on the outside. What good does it do to have youthful organs if your exterior doesn't match?"

He stood and walked over to the glass casket-sized box. "This is a modern reconstruction of Ptahmes' sarcophagus. You most likely know that his was hermetically sealed. Once the doors are closed, so is this container."

Taking off his coat, he rolled up his sleeves and put on a huge oil-skin apron. "I will mix the chemicals making up the oil which covered Ptahmes' body in the metal section. As there is air in the tank, the fluid will immediately evaporate, turning into a gas. It will seep into the glass chamber through the mesh at its bottom and fill it. You will be placed inside. That is why we took your clothes, in case you're wondering. Stripping you naked will be easier. All your flesh needs to be entirely exposed to the vapors."

"And then?"

"And then, this treatment will transform you into a living mummy. Your appearance will remain frozen in its current state: eternally youthful, handsome with an impressive physique. That is the goal of many, particularly among the higher classes and the young." He shrugged. "At least, that is my hypothesis for the treatment. It is possible you could end up resembling Ptahmes." Dr. Belleville paused a second. "I wonder if I should charge extra for this if it works?"

He walked towards three large glass jars filled with a dark, thick liquid. "I must admit, I am curious to hear your description of the experience. However, the gas created causes hallucinations. Between that and your dislike of me, you would prove to be a most unreliable narrator. Furthermore, I'm interested in discovering if the substitution process is painful; based on my previous experiments with animals, I believe it may be. To avoid any complications, I will sedate you while I observe and take notes from behind the glass."

The doctor bumped a table, and one of the castors toppled off and crashed upon his toe. Carter couldn't help but smirk. Belleville cursed like a madman and danced about the floor on one foot like a dervish, winding up by slapping Carter across his face. That gave him back his self-control. "I'll teach you to laugh at me," he growled.

He returned to his task. One by one he rolled the jars on end across the floor until all three stood beside the glass coffin. Afterwards he disappeared behind Carter's chair, returning soon, his head covered with a long breathing mask.

"I must be careful," Dr. Belleville said, his voice muffled by the mask. "These chemicals are highly volatile and flammable. I almost burned down my London house. That's why I moved here."

The sound of sweeping began again. Ptahmes back at work, Carter presumed. Dr. Belleville cursed, then waved off the interruption.

Carter watched him with passionate attention. Dr. Belleville unscrewed the stopper of the nearest jar, seized the thing in his arms and poured out half the contents into an opening in the metal portion of the coffin. A curious cloud-like steam arose that hazed the area, but soon it dissipated. The air was filled with the perfume Carter had first smelled in the cave temple of the Hill of Rakh and in his bathroom, but it was not altogether overpowering. It made his pulse throb and brought a great rush of blood to his head, hands and feet, but it did not take away his senses. Dr. Belleville, protected by his mask, was in no way affected.

He quickly unstopped the second jar, added half its contents to the first and lastly to the third. He tightly screwed a cap on the opening he had used, turned and approached Carter, removing his mask as he came. The wonderful perfume had almost died away. There was now a healthy and stimulating odor in the room that resembled boiling tar. A loud, seething, bubbling sound was plainly heard, coming from the metal tank under the glass coffin.

Dr. Belleville sat down and wiped his forehead with a handkerchief. "We must give the stuff ten minutes to mix," he said and, taking out his watch, he glanced at the time. "It's twenty past eleven. You'll begin to mummify at the half hour mark precisely, Mr. Pinsent. I shall prepare the sedative, then take care of Ptahmes." He stood up and stretched out his arms, yawning widely, and moved toward a cabinet.

As Carter's gaze remained fixed on the empty wall in front of him, he couldn't help but feel an overwhelming sense of failure. He had let down his father, May and Sir Robert. But amid the crushing weight of defeat, a strange peace settled over him. Suddenly, he was acutely aware of how small and insignificant his actions were in the grand scheme of things. And yet, there was pride in his acceptance of his present predicament—as if enduring all that pain and suffering had led him to this moment of tranquility and grace. He couldn't shake off the feeling of detachment from his surroundings, almost as if he was observing from a distance.

Dr. Belleville walked toward Carter, a syringe in one hand. Then everything went black.

CHAPTER TWENTY

"What in Hell—?" shouted Dr. Belleville.

Carter heard him rush forward, cursing angrily, then stumble and fall headlong to the floor amid a crash of glass. In the same instant, the bond around Carter's his chest suddenly relaxed, followed by the strap over his left hand. As he reached over to free his right hand, he brushed against the stump of an arm. Carter stood, stiff but quivering in every nerve.

There was a rasping sound, a match flickered to life and Dr. Belleville rose from the ruins of broken jars and test tubes. He held the light above his head, revealing Ptahmes standing next to Carter.

Dr. Belleville ripped out an oath and whipped up his revolver. There came a blinding flash and a deafening report just as the flame went out and Carter dodged to one side. "Where are you, Pinsent? Are you hurt?" he cried. "I can't have my subject damaged."

Carter did not answer. He feared that making any sound or movement would give him away… he was almost afraid to breathe. Then he wished Dr. Belleville would shoot again so that at least Carter could move under cover of the noise.

"Tell me where you are!" Dr. Belleville growled, "Or by the Lord when I catch you, I'll tear you limb from limb."

Carter breathed while the doctor spoke and ceased when he stopped.

"You can't escape me!" Dr. Belleville snarled. "I've only to light a lamp and I'll find you in a minute. But if you put me to that trouble, well, look out, that's all!"

Carter remained stock still.

"Very well," snapped Dr. Belleville. He fumbled in the darkness. Another match flared to life, casting a satanic glow on his face as he lit a bulls-eye lantern. He held it up, his revolver in the other hand. Carter sank to his hands and knees, hoping that Dr. Belleville thought he was still standing. A beam of light shot across the room, creating a moon-shaped sphere on the far wall. The light danced and flickered along every surface, tracing its way from floor to ceiling until it reached the corner. Then, in a sudden burst of intensity, it flashed back twice over the same path before attacking the next wall.

Deciding to take a calculated risk, Carter began crawling on all fours toward Dr. Belleville, like a predator stalking its prey. Each muscle in his body tensed as he inched closer and closer to his enemy, the rubberized flooring muffling the sound of his movements and the tables shielding him from view. He was determined to get within striking distance, even if it meant risking everything for the chance to take down his foe.

Dr. Belleville swung the lantern around. Ptahmes had also moved in the darkness, and now stood not three feet from the doctor. The light hit the corpse-like face and blood-red eyes. Startled, Dr. Belleville screamed and jumped back. His violent movement caused the lamp to go out, but he fired at the same time. "Damn the thing!" he growled.

Carter picked up the distinct sounds of two metal objects being placed on a table. He assumed one was the gun and the other was the lantern. The doctor tried to strike a match against the table's rough surface, but the head broke off. It sounded as though he reached for another one and scraped it along his shoe to light it. Seizing the moment, Carter quickly got behind the distracted doctor.

The lamp flickered to life again. Dr. Belleville's hand tightened around his revolver as he resumed his search, picking up the lantern. The beam from the lantern sliced through the darkness once more.

It darted and danced, like an incandescent elf, illuminating every nook and cranny, determined to find Carter. Their deadly game of keep away couldn't continue forever, and it didn't. Perhaps Carter made some sound that betrayed him to Dr. Belleville's nerve-strained senses, but Dr. Belleville uttered a savage curse and swung around to face him.

"Ha! At last!" Dr. Belleville cried as he pulled the trigger, the deafening shot narrowly missing Carter's temple. The stench of gunpowder filled the air as the smoke swirled and danced in the flickering light of the lantern. Carter lunged at his assailant, using every ounce of strength to propel the table between them like a battering ram. Just as Dr. Belleville raised his weapon to shoot again, the table made impact and sent him stumbling backwards. The lamp fell from his grasp and rolled under the table. Carter pushed with all his might against the table, and with a swift kick, managed to knock away the lantern, plunging the room into total darkness.

Carter strained to listen for any sign of movement from Dr. Belleville or Ptahmes. The room was like a pit, black and suffocating, pressing on his skin like a heavy cloak. Beads of sweat formed on his forehead as he stood rigid like a statue, breathing as quietly as he could. He couldn't see a thing. The doctor was close by, but he didn't know precisely where.

His mind raced, searching for a plan. He needed to get out of the laboratory but was disoriented in the darkness and couldn't make noise, just stumbling toward where he hoped the door was. With each passing second, his senses sharpened, attending to each subtle shift and creak within the room.

A sound, soft but blaring in the quiet of the room, caught his attention—an almost imperceptible rustling of fabric. It was coming from his left. Every instinct told him that this was Dr. Belleville, closing in on him with lethal intent... but it also could be Ptahmes. Carter edged in that direction slowly, groping through the dark, until his fingers wrapped around something cold and metal: the revolver held by Dr. Belleville.

Carter clenched the revolver tightly with both hands, determined to wrestle it away from Dr. Belleville's grip. But the doctor was just as determined, using one hand to hold onto the gun while trying to pry off Carter's grasp with the other.

As their intense grappling continued, another table was overturned, the glass laboratory equipment smashing into pieces on the floor. They fought their way over to Dr. Belleville's apparatus, knocking over the chemical jars on the floor, spilling their contents in a mess.

Carter made a desperate twist to break Dr. Belleville's grip on the revolver. The gun went off with a deafening bang, the bullet piercing the bottom tank, releasing the contents to the ground. A second shot followed, directly striking into the pool of volatile liquids.

A mass of brilliant white fire erupted with an ear-splitting roar from around the metal sarcophagus, reaching up to the ceiling in a blazing display of destruction. The fire tore through the padded lining, leaving a trail of devastation in its wake. As it reached the ceiling, it exploded into a fiery rain, showering the laboratory with sparks and embers. In mere moments, the entire place was engulfed in a raging inferno.

The heat licked at Carter, searing his skin as he fought with Dr. Belleville. The crackling flames devoured everything in their path. The air grew thick with acrid smoke, making it difficult to breathe. The struggle intensified as the two stumbled backward, their bodies crashing into the glass cabinet. It tipped over, the shattering shelves adding to the chaos. That disrupted Dr. Belleville's hold on the gun, and with one final twist from Carter, it spiraled through the air before clattering onto the scorched floorboards as the two combatants fell to the floor, rolling and punching.

Out of the raging inferno, Ptahmes emerging from the billowing smoke. The mummy moved with an unearthly determination towards Dr. Belleville. The heat of the flames whipped Ptahmes' yellow robes into a frenzy, as if fueled by a dark, otherworldly power.

Dr. Belleville scrambled to his feet, his wide eyes filled with terror as he saw Ptahmes closing in on him like a demonic apparition wreathed in fire and smoke. The mummy's skeletal fingers reached out for him, curling around his throat with a grip as unyielding as death itself.

Ptahmes' hollow eyes glowed with a malevolent red. Dr. Belleville gasped for air, his futile attempts to break free only strengthening Ptahmes' relentless grasp. With a final surge of power, the mummy dragged Dr. Belleville towards the heart of the fire. As Carter watched in horror, Ptahmes and Dr. Belleville disappeared into the inferno.

A cacophony of blood-curdling shrieks echoed through the room, drowning out even the crackling of the fire. In a burst of flames, a grotesque and burning figure emerged from the blaze. It was Dr. Belleville, his skin blistering and peeling as he frantically ran to the door. His screams pierced the air as he flung it open and stumbled through, leaving behind a trail of smoldering footprints. And just like that, the agonizing cries abruptly ceased. Carter looked back at the fire but couldn't see Ptahmes any longer. The ancient Egyptian priest had found peace at last.

Carter's mind jolted out of the shock. He sprinted towards the lab door, but then remembered the serum. Making a swift turn on his heel, he dashed back to the overturned cabinet, coughing from the thick smoke. He reached through the broken glass panel and retrieved the doctor's bag containing the precious fluid and notebook. Clutching them to his chest tightly, he dodged through the blazing flames and out of the burning laboratory.

As he stepped out of the door, he froze at the ghastly sight before him. Dr. Belleville—or what remained of him—lay splayed across a stack of wood crates, which also set them ablaze. The putrid stench of roasted flesh filled Carter's nostrils, causing him to gag and cover his mouth with one forearm.

Carter was still in the musty basement, the fire continuing to grow and consume the stacks of boxes and packing material. More bottles of chemicals, still packed, popped and shattered in the heat. Carter threw open the other door and rushed up the stairs. Bursting into the kitchen, he slammed the door behind him, hoping to contain the fire's reach. But he knew it wouldn't be enough, or for long. With each passing second, the inferno below threatened to burn through the building's supports, bringing down the entire structure. He dashed into the downstairs hallway.

"May!" he shouted. "May!"

The creak of footsteps echoed from the upstairs hall, and Carter sprinted towards the staircase. With a swift leap, he grabbed the ornate newel post and swung himself onto the first step. He started up, then stopped. Standing at the top of the stairs was Hassan Ali.

"Hassan, listen to me. The house—"

Carter never had the chance to finish the sentence. Hassan Ali lunged at him, and they both tumbled downstairs in a chaotic mess of limbs. They landed in a heap at the bottom of the stairs, with Hassan Ali on top of Carter, pinning him down.

"Listen to me!" Carter yelled, struggling to break free. "The house is on fire! Belleville is dead!"

"I do not care about Belleville. It was fated, and good riddance." Hassan Ali snatched the bag and stood. "But when he was heavy with drink, he told me what he was working on was worth much gold. It is now mine."

Hassan Ali ran towards the front door. Carter pounced after him, tackling him around the waist. The two slammed into the wall and grappled in a vicious fight, grunting and straining like wild animals battling over a fresh kill.

Carter broke free, stumbling back into a side chair. Picking it up, he swung it at his opponent. Hassan Ali ducked, and it splintered into the wall. With a primal roar, he seized Carter by the throat, his fingers digging into the flesh like claws. Carter returned the grip instantly.

With every passing second, their hands tightened around each other's necks. Carter's lungs begged for oxygen as his vision blurred and spots danced in front of his eyes. In a final attempt, he kicked out his leg, catching Hassan Ali off guard and sending them both crashing to the ground. Their grips broke and they gasped for air as they lay on the floor, panting and struggling to regain their breath.

The two staggered to stand, but Carter was quicker. He launched a heavy right hook that landed square on Hassan Ali's jaw, followed by a speedy left jab that rocked his head back. Before

Hassan could recover, Carter delivered an explosive uppercut with all of his might. Hassan Ali's eyes rolled back into his head, and he dropped to the carpet.

Scooping up the bag, Carter sprinted upstairs, taking two steps at a time. "May! May!" He stopped at the head of the stairs. "May!"

Banging came from behind the third door on his right. "Carter! In here!"

Carter rushed to the door and tried the handle. Locked. He put down the bag and looked around for the key but couldn't see one. Hassan Ali must have it.

"Get away from the door!" he bellowed.

Turning his body to the side, he aimed at the door. He charged towards it, his shoulder impacting with a thunderous boom that reverberated down the narrow hallway. The door held strong, refusing to budge. Carter stepped back and hurled himself at the door once more, the satisfying sound of wood cracking filling the air. With one final surge of energy, he flung his body at the door. It burst open and he flew through it, ending up on the floor inside the room.

May helped him to his feet. "Carter! I'm so glad to see you! What's—"

"Are you all right?"

May nodded.

Carter rushed her to the door. "Dr. Belleville is dead and the house is on fire. We need to get out of here, but I must do one thing first. Let's go."

"What? Carter—"

He took her arm and pulled her into the hallway. Picking up the bag, he gave it to her to hold. "The revival serum is inside, and Dr. Belleville's dosage notes. Now, where is Ptahmes' papyrus and stele?"

"Shouldn't we—"

"Where are they?" Carter yelled.

"Downstairs in the library," May answered. "But—"

"Take me there! Please! It's vital!"

May grabbed Carter's hand and took him down the staircase, the smell of burning wood growing stronger with each step. As they reached the bottom of the stairs, Carter found Hassan Ali missing and the front door wide open. He must have scarpered. Down the hall by the kitchen door, flames leapt and danced, devouring the back half of the house.

May opened a door and pointed. "In here. There, on the table." She coughed as the smoke rolled in.

Carter rushed through the door and lunged towards the ancient papyrus on the table. He tore at it until it was in shreds.

"What is this all about?" May asked.

"I have a promise to keep." Carter's eyes scanned the room, landing on the poker resting against the fireplace. He gripped the metal rod with both hands and swung it over his head, striking the tablet with a loud crash. Again and again, he brought down the poker until the stele was reduced to nothing but shards and dust. Finally, he flung the tool aside with a satisfied grunt. "Let's get out of here."

The two battled through the thickening, suffocating smoke, their eyes burning and watering as they clawed their way out of the front door, stopping only when they reached the side of the road. They turned back towards the house, thick black smoke billowing from it filling the sky. The fire had taken over the back of the house, licking at the walls and leaping out the windows. It was clear that nothing could be done to save the building.

"Carter, how did you get here? How did you find out? What happened Dr. Belleville? He's dead?" May fired off the questions, one after another, not waiting for answers.

He held up one hand to stop the flood of inquiries. "I will explain everything to you. The important thing is the serum in that bag will revive our fathers, pulling them out of their states of suspended animation. You are looking at living proof of its effectiveness. But right now, we should see if we can somehow summon the local fire brigade, but I doubt it will be of any help." He looked down at himself and chuckled. "Although I'm not properly dressed for a stroll into the village."

The sound of the church bell ringing reached them.

"I believe the fire brigade have noticed and are on their way." May gently placed the bag on the ground, smiled and faced Carter. She draped her arms over his shoulders and trailed her hands down his back. "I think we can find something to occupy ourselves while we wait, Mr. Pinsent."

Carter's face lit up with a grin as he slipped his arms around her waist, pulling her close. "Do you have something like this in mind, Miss Ottley?"

They kissed.

"This is most unusual." The doctor extracted the syringe from his father's arm. "I hope it works."

"It does, it does." Carter sat on the edge of the hospital bed, his eyes on his father. "It revived me from a similar state."

The doctor shook his head as he put the hypodermic needle in a metal bowl. "The story you told me was utterly fantastic. And you said all the records, the formula, for this serum are lost?"

"They were destroyed in a fire," Carter answered.

"Hopefully, there are enough trace elements in the syringe to make an analysis. According to the notes, there was just the correct dosage amounts for your father and Sir Robert." The doctor felt the pulse in Mr. Pinsent's wrist and nodded. "Heartbeat is getting stronger."

"Now expect a short seizure as he comes out of the suspended animation. It is not a major concern," Carter said. "There will be a period of some confusion, similar to when you're jolted out of from sleep."

Carter gripped his father's hand as they both watched the figure lying on the bed. Mr. Pinsent's body convulsed, then suddenly went still. The seconds ticked by slowly, feeling like hours, until finally Mr. Pinsent took a deep, hoarse breath and blinked open his eyes.

"Father?" Carter leaned over him.

Mr. Pinsent looked around the room, puzzled, then gazed at Carter. He squeezed his son's hand and smiled.

Carter grinned in return. "Welcome back, Father."

The doctor checked the pulse again. "It's strong." He addressed Mr. Pinsent. "Now, I must ask your son to leave. Then I'm going to order some food from the kitchen, followed by giving you a proper going over."

"I'll visit you tomorrow, Father." Carter stood. "I'll tell you the whole story, if you're feeling up to it."

Mr. Pinsent stopped Carter and pulled him back down. He seemed on the verge of saying something, his mouth moving as if he were trying to speak. After a moment, he managed to get some words out: "I saw her. I spoke with her."

A chill ran through Carter's body. He asked the question, although he already knew the answer. "Who?"

"Your mother." Mr. Pinsent's voice was a whisper. "She's happy and peaceful. She said we'll be united again, in God's time."

Tears stung Carter's eyes. He swallowed and choked out a response. "I'm glad to know that." He took a breath. "Now rest, listen to the doctor and do exactly what he says. I'll pop in tomorrow for a longer visit."

"I want to hear about everything." Mr. Pinsent smiled again and released Carter's hand.

Carter stepped out of the room, wiping his eyes. May stood in the corridor.

"How is your father?" she asked.

"He's revived, and seems none the worse for wear, other than he's tired." Carter chuckled. "The doctor kicked me out. And Sir Robert?"

"Also recovering." May smiled.

Carter nodded and returned the smile. "Good." He looked down at the floor. After a pause, he started awkwardly, "Do you recall the night in the library, when we worked on translating Ptahmes' message?"

"Yes."

"You told me that night that your father was all that you had in the world." Carter took May's hands in his and met her gaze. "I hope you realize that is no longer the case."

May responded with a long kiss. After the two separated, he linked his arm through hers, and they started walking down the hallway.

"And now, we are going to dine with the finest interpreter of William Shakespeare in our lifetime, Mr. Kenton Buckingham," Carter announced.

May glanced at him, confused.

"For our next project is to return Mr. Buckingham to his rightful place on the stage," Carter said. "I am hoping you know people within your circle of friends whom you could persuade to invest in such a worthwhile endeavor."

"Why, of course I do," May said with a laugh. "There's Lady Austin... and Lady Atwater... remember, you met her at the séance... oh, and Mrs. Ambrose Pratt..."

May was still reeling off names as she and Carter stepped out of the hospital into the warm sunshine.